THE AMISH FOUNDLING FINDS LOVE

EMMA CARTWRIGHT

Email: emma@emmacartwrightauthor.com

CHAPTER 1

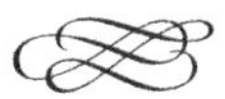

Girlish laughter echoed through the front garden, raising Martha's fair blonde head toward the porch. A blur of motion caught her attention first, then the figures came into view. Her father chased after her young daughter, his arms outstretched like a bird, lips blowing against the wind.

"*Daddi, nee*!" three-year-old Elizabeth screeched, jutting down the wooden steps toward her grandmother and mother in the garden, as if searching for protection from the raptor chasing her. Chuckling, Martha straightened herself and expanded her arms to allow for the little girl to run into her embrace.

"Your *mudder* won't save you!" Amos Hochstetler cried in a gravelly cackle. "You'll come with me back to my nest and be my little *voggel*!"

He paused to dramatically stroke his long, salt and pepper beard, extending his neck dramatically, eliciting another laugh from his granddaughter.

"Mind yourself, Amos," Martha's mother warned, wagging a slightly bent finger toward her husband. "You're liable to trip over a *henkel* doing that."

Elizabeth burst into another fit of giggles at the prospect of her grandfather falling face-first over a chicken. Amos slowed his stride, but his smile never faltered. His wife resumed her task of picking beans for dinner as Martha Fischer stroked her daughter's fine, auburn hair out of her sun-kissed face.

"I wouldn't worry about *Grossdaddi* taking you too high," she teased. "His wings don't seem to fly very well."

"He's pretending, *Mamm*," Elizabeth explained seriously. "He's not really a *voggel*."

Martha snickered again, stroking her daughter's soft cheek. "Oh, thank goodness for that," she breathed with relief. "I was worried I had lost my *vadder* to a bird too!"

Elizabeth beamed, realizing that her mother was teasing her.

"Go and wash up for *nachtesse*," she asked her child and father. "We'll be inside in a minute."

"You heard the bosses, *liebling*," Amos told the girl. "Let's go."

"Can I stay with *Mamm?*" Elizabeth insisted stubbornly, her good nature fading away with the fickleness of a toddler.

"*Grossmammi* and I will be inside soon," Martha promised. "Go wash your hands and change your dress, *pliese*."

Unexpectedly, Elizabeth stomped her foot, folding her arms defiantly over her chest. Through her peripheral vision, Martha caught her mother's shocked expression and almost laughed again.

Was it so long ago that I was a child of Elizabeth's age? Or is Elizabeth truly that much more challenging?

She inhaled deeply, prepared for the outburst.

"*Nee*!" Elizabeth protested. "I don't want to!"

"There's that infamous *Englisch* temper rearing its ugly head." Esther frowned. Martha ignored her mother's comment and crouched down to meet her child's indignant hazel eyes.

"And why not?" she asked patiently.

"I want to stay here with you," Elizabeth said again.

"I do love it when you spend your time with me," Martha agreed calmly. "But I need you to do what I ask you."

"NO!"

"Goodness," Esther grumbled, louder now so that her granddaughter could hear.

Martha paid her mother no mind at all and kept her attention fixed on her young daughter. "Then we're just wasting time, *liebling*," she explained evenly. "If you go now, like I've asked, you'll be all washed and dressed by the time I'm back inside. Then you can *hilf* with dessert for *dienacht*. But if you don't go now, you won't be able to help me with dessert because you'll be too *bissi* changing and washing your hands once I do *komme* inside."

Elizabeth's delicate nose wriggled as she considered her mother's words. "*Wat* is for dessert?" she asked suspiciously.

"Ask *Mammi*." Martha chuckled, knowing she had won this battle of the wills, at least.

"Peach cobbler," Esther announced before her granddaughter could ask. Elizabeth was out of arguments now, her bare feet flying against the grass as she zoomed back toward the house without another word of protest. Martha shook her head.

"You knew that would move her faster than a jackrabbit," the younger woman said chuckling to her mother as her father turned to race after Elizabeth.

"I would have silenced her before she got started," Esther conceded.

"I can't keep up with that *maedel*," Amos' voice was gruff with amusement. He followed Elizabeth back into the house, leaving the women alone in the garden.

"He doesn't have to push himself so hard with her," Martha reminded her mother. "He's not a spring chicken himself."

"He can use the exercise," Esther replied nonchalantly. "It keeps him *yung*. He probably remembers how he used to be with you."

A rush of affection flooded through Martha at her own childhood memories. "Unfortunately for Eliza, she didn't have the benefit of such wonderful birth parents."

Esther rose from her place in the bean patch, balancing the bowl on her hip. Her face grew serious as she regarded her only child's face. "It was Providence when that *frau* left Elizabeth on your doorstep," she reminded her daughter. "*Gott* shone on all of us that day—even if she does display some of those *Englisch* traits now and again. I'm sure time will rid her of all those issues."

Martha smiled and nodded. "Time and peach cobbler," she replied, casting off the negative thoughts that sometimes arose when she considered the circumstances which had led to the infant being abandoned on her doorstep. All children can be difficult at times, regardless of where they were born. All they required was patience and understanding.

Esther returned to the garden, bending down to pull out a weed. "I often wonder what Peter would have made of her," the older woman commented. Martha had just been thinking the same thing.

"So do I," Martha admitted, joining her mother. "Strange as it sounds, I sometimes see his characteristics in her. Of course, I know they don't share any blood, but still...sometimes, I swear I see something of him in her. Or maybe it's just wishful thinking, imagining that Elizabeth was our naturally born child."

"I don't think it's strange at all," her mother countered. "It's no coincidence that Elizabeth came to us so soon after your *mann* left this earth and that you gave her Peter's last name too, not your *vadder's*. It truly was *Gott's* hand, in all of this. He saw how heartbroken you were and sent you comfort."

Her mother's answer did not surprise Martha. She had long since learned to accept the miracle of the lost infant on her front stoop, a mere two months after her husband had passed away. Esther spoke the truth. There had been some divine intervention working on that day, meaning that Elizabeth had ended up in her life. It was small wonder that Martha could not help but ponder the event on occasion.

"You're thinking about this again because the adoption date is coming up," Esther observed astutely.

Martha nodded again. "I know."

"Don't overthink it too much, *liebling*," Esther reassured her. "This was all *Gott's* will. All we can do is live our lives the way that honors Him best."

Martha knew that too. But she could not deny that sometimes, she questioned that same will, but only in the privacy of her own head. What was it about His plan that required her beloved Peter to fall ill with motor neuron disease so young and be taken from her? How could a woman of less than thirty be left a childless widow in a community where large families are revered?

Of course, she said none of this aloud to her family. Although Martha knew her mother and father would understand her anguish, she felt shame in questioning God's ways. After all, hadn't he blessed her with Elizabeth? Perhaps that was to make up for the fact that Peter was gone and that she was now raising a child alone. But could one life really make up for another, especially when she still felt so lonely?

As if reading her mind again, Esther straightened up and glanced over her shoulder. "Have you given any thought to courting again?"

The blood drained out of Martha's face at her mother's blunt query. "*Nee*!" she rasped, turning away quickly before the blush on her cheeks was apparent. Esther laughed lightly and stepped over the cucumbers, leading her daughter out of the gate.

"*Nee*?" she repeated. "It has been three years since Peter passed away, *liebling*. You should give it some thought. Elizabeth is at an age now where she plays with other *kinner* and understands *familye* dynamics. She will want to know why she doesn't have a *vadder* and all the other *kinner* do."

"Not all the other *kinner* do," Martha protested weakly.

Esther scoffed. "*Wu* doesn't? And are you arguing that the *maedel* needs a *vadder*? Are you honestly considering having her go through life without one?"

"She has Joshua," Martha sputtered before she could think about her own words. Instantly, she regretted speaking them out loud, but it was too late to take them back.

To her horror, her mother's face lit up with more amusement. "*Yah,* she does—and so do you, if you would stop being so obstinate and allow him to court you properly. The *mann* has been hanging around for three whole years and you can't give him the time of day."

"That's not fair, *Mamm.* Joshua is a *gut mann* and a dear *freind.* Don't make it sound as if I'm cruel to him or abusing him in some way." The defensiveness in her tone wiped the smile from her mother's face.

"I don't think you have a cruel bone in your body, Martha," she replied. "All I'm saying, *liebling,* is that he is a *yung mann* and should not have to wait around for you forever. It isn't right for either of you. If you won't have him, allow him to move onto someone who will."

Inadvertently, Martha's cerulean gaze flicked toward the roadway, across the blooming Ohio fields, toward the neighboring farmland. Joshua Troyer's land was not quite visible from where she stood, but she took comfort in knowing that he was never far away from her when she needed him. The notion of him marrying someone else did not sit well with her, but the idea of being courted was almost as unappealing. She constantly felt stuck in a place where no choice seemed right.

"The questions will only grow harder as Elizabeth gets older," Esther continued. "She will want to know about her *Englisch familye,* too. It's best that you give her the most solid foundation you can now—and before you lose a *gut mann,* Martha."

Unhappiness twitched inside Martha at the reminder. These were all facts that she had considered herself before committing to the legal adoption, but now that they were becoming a reality, it was all too much on her shoulders. Perhaps she had believed there would be a few more years before it all came to a head.

"It wouldn't be much of a stretch," Esther added when her daughter did not respond. "Joshua is here almost every day already. Elizabeth adores him, and he was Peter's best friend."

"Isn't that the problem, though?" Martha muttered more to herself than to her mother. They climbed the wide steps to the wraparound porch and paused before entering the screen door.

"Peter wanted you taken care of. He told your father and Joshua as much before he passed. You must let go of whatever it is that's keeping you from having a good, full life. Not just for yourself, but for Elizabeth, too."

Exhaling deeply, Martha nodded her head. Esther reached up with her free hand to cup her daughter's pretty face. "You are so *yung*," she said softly. "You have your whole life ahead of you. Joshua can make you happy. Give him a chance."

The screen door flew open before Martha could respond, her small daughter appearing in a fresh dress, her hands extended. "I'm clean!" she declared proudly, twirling around. "Peach cobbler, *pliese*!"

Laughing, the women nodded, heading into the house to make supper for the overeager child and her grandfather.

As her mother retreated to the kitchen with Elizabeth, Martha lingered in the hallway, lost in thought as she mulled over her mother's sage advice.

There was no doubt that Joshua Troyer had exercised extreme patience with her over the past three years, catering to her needs the best he could while managing his own farm. As her mother had stated, the man came by almost every day, whether to help Amos with the livestock or to simply do fixtures around the house. And he asked for nothing in return, but his interest was known.

Elizabeth looked forward to his visits, and he always had a kind word for the little girl. Like everyone else in the community, Joshua had watched her grow up under Martha's loving care. He often appeared with a handcrafted toy for her, and Elizabeth genuinely adored the man.

Martha wished she could learn to care for him as much as he cared for her.

But I never will learn how unless I try, she reasoned, starting toward the kitchen to rejoin the rest of her family. *Mamm is right. It has been long enough and Eliza deserves more.*

Esther looked up from the counter when she entered, a curious smile on her face. "Are you all right?" she asked, carrying on with her chopping. At her side, Elizabeth sloppily beat eggs in a bowl, bringing a genuine smile to Martha's face.

"*Yah,*" she replied honestly. "I am."

Her life was good. She should not create sadness where there was nothing but light. It was time to move forward. Her mother was right. It's what her husband would have wanted, and Elizabeth deserved a father, too.

CHAPTER 2

Dust particles danced through the streaming sunlight as Joshua sanded the surface lightly, blowing the excess residue aside. His calloused hands ran over the smooth surface, and he sat back to admire his handiwork. He hoped the Hochstetlers would be pleased with his latest creation when he presented it to them later, after he had finished staining it.

The thought of the Hochstetlers immediately turned his mind toward Martha and he lifted his head to figure out the time. His dark eyes turned to the outside light, gauging the afternoon sun for a hint of the hour of the day. As if on cue to his thought, his mother's voice rang out from the house, summoning him for supper.

Oh no. I have spent too long out here this afternoon.

Regret shot through him, and he sighed. Wiping off the surface of the armoire, Joshua brushed his hands against his dirty pants and headed toward his family's home, just over the hill from his workspace. His father's buggy had not returned from the furniture shop where they worked together most days.

"Where is *Daed?*" Joshua asked his younger siblings as he entered the house. The three youngsters glanced up from their place on the living room floor where they were involved in a game of Chutes and Ladders.

"Not *deheem* yet," his youngest sister explained. "He should be here soon."

The smell of roasted meat and steamed vegetables reached his nose as he ambled toward the main floor bathroom to wash his hands before joining his mother in the kitchen.

"We're not going to *esse* without *Daed*, are we?" he asked, again glancing out the window.

Anna Troyer shook her head and laughed. "*Nee*, of course not." "But he should be *deheem* any minute. The shop closed half an hour ago."

For the first time in hours, Joshua's eyes found their way to the clock in the corner of the kitchen. Disappointment set in as he realized how late it had gotten.

"What's wrong, *sohn?*" Anna asked, catching her oldest son's expression. "Did you not get your *warrick* done today?"

Joshua shook his head and sat in one of the sturdy wood island chairs his father had built as his mother pulled fresh bread from the oven. "I got enough done," he replied. "But I lost track of time, like I always do when I *warrick* from home." He laughed hollowly, his eyes trailing out toward the window, across the fields toward the roadway.

Anna smiled openly as she recognized her son's problem.

"Ah. You were hoping to stop by the Hochstetlers and see Martha Fischer before *nachtesse,* weren't you?"

Embarrassed, Joshua lowered his gaze. "I only want to see if they need anything," he mumbled.

"I know, Josh. You're a *gut bu,* always taking care of that *frau.* Peter was right to leave her in your hands."

Heat rose up the base of Joshua's neck at the mention of his lost friend, a smidgen of guilt accompanying the mention of Martha in the same sentence. "I do what I can between *warrick*. I don't know if it's enough."

"I'm sure Martha appreciates all the *hilf* she can get. Her family are *gut* people, but like me and your *vadder,* they had their *kinder*. They don't have the same energy they did when they were *yung*. And I'm sure raising an *Englisch kin* comes with its own set of challenges."

Defensiveness struck in Joshua. "Eliza is a *gut maedel,*" he protested. "No worse than Miriam at the same age."

"I can hear you!" his little sister called from the living room floor and Joshua grinned impishly as his mother snorted, setting the loaf down to cool.

"Am I wrong?" he insisted as Anna chuckled.

"Martha is doing a *wunderbar* job with that *kin,* but I wonder where she would be if it weren't for your help. Sometimes I think she bit off more than she can chew when she agreed to that adoption. She has no idea where that baby came from."

Anna shook her head.

Joshua did not want Martha thinking of him as her savior, her friend. He hoped by now that she would be looking at him with more interest in her eyes.

"Have you asked her about a courtship?" Anna questioned, pausing to wipe her hands on her apron. Spreading her palms over the butcher block, she peered inquisitively at her son's avoiding eyes. "Joshua?"

"She needed time to heal after Peter's passing. His illness was long and hard on her," he reminded her.

"It was long and hard on everyone," Anna countered. "Including you."

"Which is why I understand her need for time," Joshua said quietly. "I am willing to wait for her as long as it takes."

"What if she's never ready, Josh? She has that *maedel* now. Maybe the idea of remarriage isn't in her mind at all now that she is so focused on Elizabeth."

Joshua admitted silently that he had often had the same thoughts. Any time he had tried to broach the subject of marriage with Martha, it seemed the topic invariably circled back to that of Elizabeth. Joshua was never sure if it was purposeful or if Martha was simply overburdened with her motherhood duties. And he was too gentle to push.

"The *maedel* needs a *vadder*," he answered firmly, refusing to give up on Martha. "Every *kin* needs a *vadder*."

"I just wouldn't want to see you wasting your efforts on someone who won't have you. Then you will be too *auld* to start a *familye* of your own and then where will you be?" Anna pressed. "As much as you care about that *frau*, I want you to think about yourself too, Josh. I like Martha, but you are my *sohn*."

"*Mamm*, Martha and I will be together," Joshua insisted, his gut tightening at her concerns.

"When?"

He did not like the challenge in her tone, but before he could respond, the back door opened and his father ambled through. Joshua exhaled a breath as his mother and father greeted one another, his mind whirling.

She isn't wrong, he thought unhappily. *I shouldn't be willing to wait around forever.*

But even as he thought it, he knew that he would do exactly that if that was what Martha required of him. He was in love with Martha Fischer and if he had to wait forever, so be it.

Twilight oranges filtered through Geauga County, covering Sugar Lake in a translucent, summery glow. Succulent flower aromas permeated the air, and Joshua could not resist stopping to pick a small bouquet on his way across the country roadside.

His siblings' distant voices in the yard of his house where they played faded further as he moved toward the Hochstetler's land until it was replaced by Elizabeth's sweet singing.

The little girl sat in a wooden swing, hanging from the front of the house, her tiny legs dangling awkwardly over the sides as she sang to herself. Her hazel eyes brightened immediately to see her neighbor.

"Josh!" she cooed, extending her arms toward him. Joshua hurried forward, not realizing that Amos Hochstetler sat on the porch, watching over his granddaughter until he had the child in his arms.

"There you are!" Amos boomed heartily. His voice spun Joshua around and he greeted the older man with a smile.

"*Hallo* Amos! I didn't see you there."

"I didn't think we'd see you today. Usually, you *komme* earlier than this."

Elizabeth slung her arms around the young man's neck as he carried her toward the front door.

"I lost track of time," he admitted. "But your armoire is done. I just need to stain it."

Pleasure illuminated Amos' face as Joshua handed the little girl to him. Elizabeth easily climbed into her grandfather's lap and he accepted her with open arms. Amos nodded at the bouquet in Joshua's hands. "Are those for me?" he joked, and Joshua flushed crimson.

"*Nee…*" He glanced at Elizabeth as she exclaimed, "They're for *Mamm,* of course."

The child slipped off her grandfather's lap and extended her chubby hands eagerly to take the flowers.

"What do you say, Eliza?" Amos chided her.

"*Denki!*"

"Go find your *Grossmammi* and have her put those in *wasser,*" Amos instructed. Obligingly, Elizabeth scampered off to do what she was told, leaving the men alone on the porch.

"Did you need me to do anything today?" Joshua asked. "Even though I'm late."

Amos shook his head vehemently. "*Komme. Hoch dich anne,*" he urged, gesturing for the younger man to sit, and Joshua obliged, perching in the neighboring chair. "There's *nix* for you to do here *dienacht* but relax. I'll have Martha bring you a *kaffe*."

Joshua shook his head before Amos could call out to his daughter, leaning forward in his place. "Before you do," he said, lowering his voice confidentially. "I was hoping to have a private moment with you."

Interest piqued, Amos sat forward also, cocking his head to the side. "What is on your mind, Josh?"

Clearing his throat delicately, Joshua looked back toward the house, ensuring that no one was within earshot before he continued his innermost thoughts.

"I have been giving a lot of thought to asking Martha for a proper courtship," he confessed. "It has been three years since Peter's death, and I feel as if she might be ready to move on now."

The grandfather pursed his lips together pensively, sitting back to fold his hands over his chest for a moment.

"You know you don't need to ask my permission," Amos told him.

"*Nee,* I know that," Joshua agreed. "But I would like your opinion on the matter."

To his disappointment, Amos did not respond. "You think it's too soon?" Joshua sighed, his hopes dissipating as he read the expression on Amos' face.

"*Nee*!" Amos laughed. "Not at all. In fact, Esther and I pray about this every night, that Martha will overcome her grief and sadness, and move on with her life."

Joshua waited, sensing that there was more.

"But it isn't up to us," he continued. "It is up to her and to *Gott*."

Joshua nodded, staring down at his hands, unsure of what to say now. He had hoped for a ringing endorsement from Amos, a vote of confidence. Instead, he felt more conflicted than ever on his next moves.

"However," Amos went on. "There is only one way to move on. And that it to live your life without being affected by the ghost of the past, *yah*?"

The younger man shot his companion a sidelong look. "*Wat* do you suggest I do to *hilf* Martha move forward?"

Amos smiled enigmatically. "The only thing you can do, really," he replied. "You will have to ask her to be courted."

Baffled by the full circle of the conversation, Joshua gaped at him. "But you said—"

"I said that only she can decide, but sometimes what people need is the reminder that the option is still there. Perhaps both of you have gotten a little too…stagnant in your relationship. Maybe she sees you only as a *freind* now because you've only ever acted like one."

"What if she refuses?" Joshua asked slowly and Amos snorted, unbothered by his question.

"Then it won't be anything you haven't heard before," he answered.

He does have a point there.

"But if it helps at all, I do believe that she will be more receptive now than before," Amos volunteered.

"Why do you say that?" Joshua was not convinced, but he trusted Martha's father enough to hear him out entirely.

"There's a loneliness in her now that wasn't there before. I think she recognizes that Eliza is getting older and needs a *vadder*, siblings. And that she needs a *mann*, a partner."

Amos smiled kindly, leaning forward again. "You have been so good to her and to our *familye* since Peter died, Joshua. Esther and I would like nothing more than for you to be a part of our *familye* in the real sense. It will not be much of an extension in our eyes."

"I'd like that too," Joshua told him earnestly.

"Now all you have to do is convince Martha," he concluded.

Both men watched the remnants of the sun slip fully away beyond the Sugar Lake town limits, embracing them in a bath of blue light. Crickets chirped nearby, echoing the mournful call of a loon. The serenity of the moment was not lost on the younger man, and Joshua wished he was sharing this moment with Martha instead of her father.

Next time, he vowed he would bring the flowers directly to her.

CHAPTER 3

As they had done the last few times, all the district turned up for Elizabeth's third adoption day celebration. They came armed with casserole dishes and pie plates, covering the folding tables with sweet-smelling treats and baked goods from all over. Buggies lined the entire Hochstetler property, spilling off the gravel driveway and onto the lone country road.

Children flocked around the little girl, cooing over her new dress, which Martha had spent several evenings making over the past two weeks. It was such a small gesture, but it gave her daughter such pleasure, skipping along in her purple "grownup" dress with the other older girls. The sun shone brightly overhead, commemorating the best day of Martha's life.

"I can't believe it's been three years since she arrived," one of her long-time friends commented, following Martha's gaze as she trailed after the miracle who was her daughter. "It feels like just yesterday, doesn't it?"

"I know," Martha agreed. "Sometimes I can't believe how fast she has grown. Time does fly when you have a *kin*. You really don't understand it until it happens to you."

Her companion chuckled and gestured toward her own two children nearby. "You don't have to tell me, Martha. Ten years happened in the blink of an eye. Soon, we'll be as *auld* as our *leit.*"

She laughed. "It goes faster when you have more," her companion added with a knowing nudge, nodding toward Joshua Troyer, who stood a few feet away, watching them. "Maybe it's time to consider growing your blessed little *familye* too."

Martha's cheeks burned at her friend's blatant suggestion, her blonde head turning to avoid Joshua's overt stare. She had to admit that she, too, was attracted to the man. Yet overcoming the guilt and grief was proving to be a much more difficult task than she ever imagined.

"You really should think about Joshua Troyer before someone else does," her friend urged, alarming Martha. She whipped her head toward her friend suspiciously.

She's the second person to say that to me. Is Joshua showing interest in someone else?

"Do you know if he's been speaking to someone else?" she asked, trying to sound innocent. Her friend chortled again.

"I haven't heard yet," she warned. "But I wouldn't be surprised if I were to hear something soon."

Martha knew she could not fault him if he was. The man had been inordinately patient with her for far too long. But how would she ever bear it if he actually married another?

The question haunted her throughout the gathering. Simultaneously, she wondered if she could fully commit herself to him now, even after all this time. They had been friends for so long, it almost seemed strange to venture into another avenue.

Or was she just making more excuses again?

This is not the day for such questions, she chided herself. *This is Elizabeth's day, not mine.*

Her daughter relished in the attention of her third adoption date.

"I'm three now, *Mamm,*" she announced proudly as the party wound to a close, the afternoon sunshine spilling lower over the horizon. Sleepiness hooded her sweet hazel eyes, the lack of an afternoon nap clearly affecting her today.

"*Yah, liebling,* you're growing so fast," Martha agreed, scooping her up to hold against her shoulder. "Soon, I won't be able to carry you anymore. You'll just be too heavy."

Elizabeth giggled. "That's okay," she declared. "Joshua can carry me then. He's got big muscles."

Her grandmother overheard the little girl's proclamation as Martha set the child back down on her feet and ambled closer when Elizabeth scurried off to play. "Do you see? She already regards him as a father figure in some ways."

"That's because he's always here," Martha replied patiently.

"Exactly my point," Esther pressed. "Why not make it more formal?"

Martha did not want to have this discussion with her mother or anyone else while there was cleaning to be done. She picked up empty plates and dishes from the table, seeing off the neighbors until only a few people remained behind, chatting with Amos.

Among them was Joshua, but his family had long since retired to their home.

"I'll fold the tables and put the chairs away," he volunteered.

"*Denki*, Josh," Martha said appreciatively. Her mother had taken Elizabeth inside to ready herself for bedtime. She continued to tidy up the dishes and food as Joshua worked silently a few feet away. She pretended not to notice as he snuck glances at her every time he passed by. But she silently admitted she was grateful for his presence. If not for him, the past few years would have been too quiet and lonely. He had been her one constant all along.

He truly has been my rock, my foundation for several years. I'm not being fair to him.

"That was a nice gathering," Joshua commented, rejoining her after he had finished the task. By now, the sun had fully set over the houses and no one remained on the property, Amos disappearing into the house to join his wife.

"It was. A good turnout. I'm glad so many people came," Martha agreed, genuinely pleased. "It surprises me that they still bother, even after three years."

"The entire community adores Eliza." Joshua chuckled lightly, leaning against the garden gate as Martha smoothed the front of her dress. She was suddenly nervous, as if she could sense the difference in Joshua despite their lighthearted, common conversation. "It's no surprise that they always turn up for her. It's not every day that we get an infant left for us to raise."

"I suppose," she agreed, catching his eyes. Her smile faded as his expression turned serious. She shifted her weight uncomfortably from one foot to the other, her blonde head lowered as an awkward silence fell between them.

"Martha..." Joshua began tentatively, and she inhaled slowly. "I have been waiting patiently for you to heal from the pain of Peter's passing for three years now. I've tried to be at your side all through the adoption process with Elizabeth, to *hilf* your *familye...*" he trailed off and cleared his throat. "Maybe I didn't do as much as I could—"

"You have been a *wunderbar freind* to me, Josh," Martha interjected quickly.

He paused, his eyes trailing over her face.

"I was hoping that maybe you could learn to see me as something more than that," he admitted, speaking the words that Martha had known were coming for a long time already.

She pursed her lips, the memory of her fears, her mother's warning that he would not be there forever, echoing through her mind. But she could not bring herself to nod, not yet.

"I wouldn't think of pressuring you," he added quickly. "I only want to see if you'll join me on Friday for the singing. I could pick you up?"

The offer hung between them like stale campfire smoke, and Martha's impulse was to refuse. She stopped herself before she could, weighing the options of breaking Joshua's heart when he had waited so long to ask her.

He might never ask again, and then wat? Will he give up? Will he stay away because of embarrassment? Will I ruin our friendship?

That alternative was unbearable for Martha. She could not lose Peter and Joshua, too.

"You're not ready." He sighed heavily.

"*Nee,* it's not that!" Martha fibbed, feeling even worse now that she was lying to her dear friend. "I-I am trying to remember if there are already plans on Friday evening. I thought my *leit* had mentioned something..."

She coughed at the lie, averting her gaze so he would not see it, her cheeks crimson.

"My *leit* would be happy to watch Eliza if your parents are *bissi,*" Joshua offered. More shame overwhelmed her, but she still could not bring herself to agree to the date. The concession stuck to the roof of her mouth like molasses.

"Let me check with them, all right?" she breathed, noting the deep disappointment on his face. "I'll let you know what they say in the *mariye.*"

Joshua nodded, but his sadness was palpable. Even if he had not outright read the lie, he could see she was not excited. Martha had not given him the response he had been hoping for. "I should head *deheem,*" he murmured, turning toward the driveway, leading back to the road.

"*Denki* for all your *hilf*...again," she breathed, hearing how futile her gratitude sounded now, even to her own ears.

He nodded again without turning around, his dejected, hunched shoulders the last thing she saw as he retreated toward his property across the fields.

"Did you really let him go?" Esther's voice cut out through the evening light the moment that Joshua was out of earshot, her disapproval tangible. Martha whirled around, her heart in her throat as she realized her mother had been standing on the porch, watching the whole time. Esther stood with her hands on her hips.

"*Mamm*, it's not polite to eavesdrop," she chided, gliding up the steps of the porch. She was grateful for the lowlight, her cheeks almost purple with humiliation now.

"Do you not want to remarry, Martha? Do you want to be alone forever?"

"*Mamm*—"

"You will never find a better *mann* that Joshua Troyer. And once he is gone, he will not *komme* back. You must know that."

Martha froze in her place. She turned to look at her mother suspiciously. "You keep saying that. Is there someone else? Has he shown interest in another *frau*?"

Esther's face pinched into a scowl. "If you don't want him for a *mann*, why do you care?"

The question twisted Martha's indecisive stomach in knots.

Dear Gott, why are you making this choice so difficult for me? I truly care for Joshua, but as a mann? Can I ever learn to see him that way?

"For Joshua's sake, I hope he is able to move on. He deserves happiness...and so do you, *liebling*."

Martha spun back around and sprinted toward the roadway, ignoring her mother's calls behind her. "Where are you going now? It's late!"

She rushed toward the Troyer household, catching up with Joshua just as he reached the back of his property line.

"Josh!" she gasped breathlessly.

Shocked, he whirled around, his eyes narrowing in the darkness. "*Wat* is it? What's wrong?" he asked in alarm, searching her over. "Are you all right?"

Pausing to catch her breath, one hand on her heart, Martha held up a hand.

"Goodness, Martha, did something happen to Eliza? Your *leit*?" he begged, rushing to her aid. In that moment, Martha was granted a burst of clarity. Even in his deepest despair, Joshua was not worried about his own feelings, but hers. She would be a fool not to consider a future with him. She had been a fool to wait as long as she had. At once, she realized what she had to do.

"Everyone is fine," she managed to rasp, straightening herself. "I wanted to catch you before you got *deheem*."

Confusion colored his handsome face, and he peered at her with bewilderment.

"To give you my answer about Friday," she continued. "Before you got home."

His worry gave way to disappointment again. "It's all right—"

"I would like to go to the singing with you," she blurted out before she could change her mind again.

Shock and genuine pleasure overtook Joshua's complexion. "*Yah*? Really?" he choked.

"*Yah…*" she mumbled, suddenly unsure again, but Joshua immediately picked up on her uncertainty.

Tentatively, he reached for her hand. To her horror, she realized her palms were clammy, yet she did not pull away as he kept his distance. "I promise we will move slowly," he whispered. "We will not discuss anything you're not ready for."

Relief swept through Martha, and she nodded gratefully. She did not know why she had been so nervous. Of course, Joshua would always be a perfect gentleman.

"I know, Josh."

They shared another smile.

"I should get *deheem*. I didn't tell my *mudder* where I was going—although I'm sure she could guess."

"I'll walk you back," he offered, releasing her hand. Another wave of thankfulness washed over Martha as she realized just how fortunate she truly was.

God was so good.

CHAPTER 4

Joshua's brow furrowed as Caleb Miller laid out the plan in front of him. "It's going to take that long?" he asked, smothering his disappointment. "A whole month? The summer will be over by then and then when will I court Martha?"

The buggy maker chuckled dryly, raising a bushy eyebrow. "Well, if you'd been sensible and ordered it when you first started showing an interest in the *frau,* it would have been ready years ago," he teased. "But since you waited too long, here we are."

Joshua ignored the comment and pursed his lips. "I realize you have other orders ahead of mine, but I would be very appreciative if you could finish my *waegel* ahead of schedule. I'll pay more, of course."

Caleb's beam widened, his eyes twinkling. "I will move some things around and see what I can do. I have always had a soft spot for *yung lieb.* Frankly, the whole district has been hoping for you and Martha to get together. It's high time she found a *vadder* for that little girl."

Joshua's face warmed at the characterization of their relationship. "I wouldn't go announcing the banns yet," he mumbled.

"All in due time," Caleb agreed with a laugh. "I'll call on you when it's done. But don't go holding your breath too much."

Thanking him, Joshua left the carriage maker's shop and headed into the brilliant summer day. Logically, he knew he should not be disappointed by the amount of time it would take, but he had been hoping to impress Martha with the new buggy sooner rather than later.

He had walked into Sugar Lake that morning, leaving his family's buggy back at the furniture store, where his father was manning the business for the moment. Joshua had a little time to enjoy the day and plan out the rest of his evening with Martha. Little else had consumed his thoughts all day.

In truth, Joshua had been planning the event in his mind for three years, his affections for his best friend's wife existing even before Peter had passed. Even as children, Joshua had been awed by Martha's patience and kindness. It had shone through in the way she took care of his ailing friend and the abandoned baby on her doorstep. The more time Joshua spent around Martha, the more he fell in love with her. He needed to ensure that everything he did with her from here out was perfect, outlining his feelings for her.

But I won't push her, no matter what.

Friday could not come fast enough, the week dragging on as he continued to abide by his chores and help out at the furniture store. He had finally applied the last coat of stain to the armoire and intended to deliver it to the Hochstetlers on Friday, the piece finished well ahead of schedule.

By the time he circled back to the furniture store in the center of downtown Sugar Lake, he was excited again about the upcoming date. His father immediately noted the animation on his face.

"You made it back," Abraham joked when he laid eyes on his son. "I was beginning to think maybe your singing was *heit,* and you had forgotten about *warrick* today."

Joshua grinned and slipped his rubber apron back on. "When have I ever forgotten about *warrick?*" he challenged lightly. "And the singing is on Friday, not tonight"

"I am well aware of when the singing is," Abraham replied dryly, picking up his ledger book and resuming his work. "You've been talking about *nix* else since you returned from Elizabeth's gathering on Saturday. I don't even think you heard a word during worship on Sunday. The deacon was looking directly at you and you were off in dreamland."

"He was not!" Joshua cried indignantly.

"He was," Abraham countered without losing his smile. "But I don't think anyone can fault you for being so lost in the clouds."

Joshua regarded his father with veiled eyes as he busied himself with the display inventory.

"It's been a long wait," he admitted when his father did not add anything to his thoughts. "I want to make sure I do everything properly."

"You are a *gut mann, sohn,*" Abraham informed him bluntly. "Martha knows that. You don't have to impress her. That is perhaps the beauty of your relationship already. There is no real need for this courtship, since you know one another so well."

A small frown formed over Joshua's face as he considered his father's words.

But that's not entirely true, is it? he mused silently. *We have spent so much time together over the years, but how much do we really know about one another personally?*

Yes, he was aware what kind of wife and mother Martha was, but as a person, he knew very little. And vice versa. Martha had known him since childhood, yet they had not attended Rumspringa together or spent time in the same circle of friends. She knew him as the helpful neighbor, not the man who enjoyed fishing and hiking.

A spark of excitement illuminated within him at the prospect of learning more about Martha. He was not sure he could wait until Friday to see her now.

"Josh!" Amos cried happily as he pulled the family wagon up to the Hochstetler property. The older man trudged down the front steps to greet him. Joshua realized that the entire family always seemed pleased to see him whenever he arrived.

Is that why I'm always so happy to be here? Because it feels so comfortable around Esther and Amos, and Elizabeth, too?

It certainly helped that he got along so well with Martha's family. Perhaps his father was right. The transition would be quite smooth if they ever decided to marry.

If Martha ever got to that point.

Amos' eyes brightening at the sight of the massive wooden piece strapped to the back of the buggy. "You brought the armoire!"

"It's finally ready," Joshua confessed, peeking toward the house for a glimpse of Martha. Amos caught his covert glance and grinned.

"She's putting Elizabeth to bed, but I'm sure she'll be along soon. Let me *hilf* you with that."

Together, they unloaded the armoire, hoisting it carefully over the wooden steps toward the front door and into the house. Esther appeared, her face lighting up at the sight.

"Joshua!" she exclaimed. "You brought the dresser!"

Her excited call brought Martha to the top of the stairs and Joshua set the armoire down to wipe a bead of sweat from his brow, guilt sweeping through him as he realized he might be waking the child. "Maybe we should leave it down here for now if the *bobbli* is sleeping," he suggested.

"*Nee, nee,*" Martha chuckled. "That *maedel* will sleep through a tornado. You should know that by now."

Joshua shrugged and snickered. "*Yah,* I suppose you're right," he agreed.

"*Komme,* I'll *hilf* you guide it up the stairs. They've been counting the days for this to arrive," Martha urged, gesturing for him to come the rest of the way up the steps. "I don't want to hear any more about this armoire."

Nodding, Joshua and Amos lifted the heavy, well-crafted piece the rest of the way until they had it firmly situated in the master bedroom.

"You and your *vadder* do such *gut warrick*," Esther breathed appreciatively. "Such craftsmanship."

"Josh did this himself," Martha said unexpectedly.

He turned and looked at her curiously. "How did you know?" Joshua was sure he had not mentioned he was handling it on his own.

A pink tinge touched Martha's fair cheeks, and she turned away, only her profile visible. "Oh…I can tell," she murmured. "You and your *vadder* have different styles."

Joshua was unexpectedly pleased by her observation. He had been trained in the craft by his father. It had never occurred to him that he had his own unique way of building, let alone that it was distinctive enough to be noticed by anyone.

"I can't tell," Esther admitted, but her confession did not diminish Joshua's elation. Martha could tell, and that was all that mattered.

Does she notice little things about me? I never thought she would.

"*Komme* downstairs," Esther urged. "I'll make some *kaffe* and I have fresh baked *eepie*. But don't tell Elizabeth you're eating her cookies."

Chuckling, they headed back down the steps, and back out onto the porch as Esther gathered refreshments. Several chickens hurried by as they sat overlooking the garden, squawking loudly as they chased one another.

Joshua stole a look at Martha and she returned his gaze evenly, causing his pulse to quicken.

"You really didn't have to make a special trip out here, *dienacht*," Amos told the young man. "You could have delivered this on Friday when you were *cooma*."

He looked meaningfully at his daughter, who smiled.

"It's no trouble," Joshua reassured him. "We only just live across the way, remember?"

"We remember," Amos agreed with a chortle.

Esther pushed open the screen door with her foot, carrying a tray with coffee and cookies. Her daughter jumped up to help her, setting the refreshments on the table. She deliberately handed Joshua a mug, her eyes lingering over his as he accepted the drink, and Joshua was glad he had come.

Little steps in the right direction, he thought. *But we will get there.*

On Friday, the night of the singing, Elizabeth pitched a fit because she was unable to attend with her mother and Joshua. It was the first time in the child's memory that she was being left alone while her mother went out without her.

"I want to go too!" the toddler wailed, stomping her foot as her mother tried to leave with Joshua. "Why can't I go too, *Mamm*?!"

At first, Joshua was concerned that Martha might relent to her daughter's tactics, but Martha was smooth and relentless.

"Tonight is just for grownups," Martha explained patiently, as Joshua waited at the base of the porch stairs. Martha crouched down at her daughter's level, speaking in an even tone. "Sometimes, grownups want to do things on their own, without *kinner*, Eliza."

Elizabeth's wide eyes flooded with tears and she flailed her arms against her mother's chest. Easily and unaffected, Martha wrapped the girl up in her own arms, hugging her close until the tantrum subsided. Joshua could hardly believe how incredibly patient she was.

"Are you quite finished?" Martha murmured as Elizabeth sniffled and whined.

"I want to *komme* too!"

"Your fussing won't make me bring you," Martha told her evenly. "But you are making us late for the singing. It's rude to interrupt people when they have already begun. Is that what you'd like?"

Uncertainly, Elizabeth stepped back and eyed her mother, as if weighing what another outburst might achieve. "*Nee*..." the child drawled slowly.

"Go on," Esther grunted, dropping her hands on the child's shoulders. "I'll deal with this one."

"*Denki, Mamm,*" Martha told her gratefully. "*Pliese* be *gut* for *Grossmammi* and *Daddi*, Eliza."

Pouting, Elizabeth said nothing as Joshua waved goodbye and escorted Martha toward the waiting buggy.

"*Kinner,*" he chuckled when they had loaded onto the buckboard and started toward Sugar Lake to catch the beginning of the singing. "They're all difficult at that age."

Incredulously, Martha cast him a sidelong look. "Are they? My *mudder* is convinced Eliza has an *Englisch* temper.'"

Joshua had heard his own parents suggest the same thing about Elizabeth, but he did not confirm this to Martha. "You don't have younger siblings, but I do. I can confirm they are all cranky and impatient between the ages of two and four. There is simply something in their development that makes them want to be *gruuft*."

He balked as he caught Martha's sidelong look. "Not that I'm saying Eliza is an imp—she's quite good compared to my own siblings, even at that age."

Martha giggled, her shoulders relaxing. "She can be a *gruuft*," she confessed in a low voice. "But she is my *gruuft* and not very often. I believe with God's grace and our community's love, she will overcome whatever genetics she was born into."

It was Joshua's turn to give her a sidelong look. "You never learned anything about her real parents? At all?"

The smile faded, and Joshua was instantly contrite. "We don't have to talk about it if you don't want to. I didn't mean to bring it up, Martha."

She shook her head and met his eyes with an uneasy smile.

"*Nee,* I don't mind talking about it," Martha reassured him. "I think about it from time to time, where she came from, who her parents were and how they saw fit to leave her in the country, without knowing anything about who took her in."

Joshua said nothing, his ears merely listening. There was no judgement in Martha's tone, only genuine sadness and curiosity. "I often wonder what terrible situation they must have been in for that to happen. What kind of situation brings someone to do something like that?"

"But for the adoption to be legal, the *Englisch* system must have some idea of who the parents are, don't they?"

"If they do, I have learned nothing. All I know is that the *bobbli* is mine according to their courts."

"And to *Gott*," Joshua added.

She beamed. "*Yah*. And to *Gott*, of course."

"Whoever her parents were, they aren't her parents anymore," Joshua added quietly. "You are her mother now. The only *mudder* she's ever known and will ever know."

Her eyes lingered on his face and his heart skipped a beat as he read her innermost thoughts—or he hoped he did.

And maybe, I am going to be Elizabeth's father too.

CHAPTER 5

It seemed that Joshua's concern for the completion of his buggy was unwarranted. There was no need to impress Martha, and his father was always happy to permit his son the use of the family's carriage whenever Martha agreed to an evening out. Saturdays were for picnics and Fridays for singings or community events. The young widow never rejected his offers and the more time they spent together, the more she relaxed around him, lowering her inhibitions more on the subject of marriage.

Every other Sunday, both families would join together and drive to worship and share in dinner in the evening.

Joshua looked forward to the family affairs almost as much as he did the time he spent alone with Martha. More and more, they were growing to respect one another as more than friends, as potential partners, in marriage one day.

"Careful, *liebling*," Martha called out to her daughter from her place on the gingham blanket. "Not too close to the *wasser, pliese*."

Elizabeth heeded her mother's warning, keeping her distance from the pond's edge as she threw the edges of her sandwich toward the ducks, giggling as they quacked for more.

"She has a way with the animals, doesn't she?" Joshua commented admiringly, watching as a tiny duckling ambled closer, wanting to take food directly from the child's hand.

"*Yah,* and she loves horses," Martha conceded. "The other day, I couldn't find her and when I did, she was curled up in the stables."

Joshua laughed aloud, envisioning the sweet redheaded child doing exactly that. "When she's old enough, I'll teach her how to ride properly," he promised.

"She might be teaching us at the rate she's growing," Martha replied dryly. "I see the way she eyes the horses, as if she might try when no one is looking. I told my *vadder* to keep a good eye on her."

Her daughter scampered back toward them, happiness shining in her pretty face.

"More *brot, pliese,*" she begged, holding out her hand for more bread.

"You've fed the *voggel* more than you've eaten yourself," Martha chided her, but relented and handed her more bread crusts.

"They're *hungerich, Mamm,*" the child explained before dashing off to scatter more crumbs for the birds.

"She plays with the animals because she doesn't have any siblings," Joshua commented, avoiding her gaze. He spread his legs out to stare toward the sparkling lily pond, his peripheral vision catching a frog leaping from one pad to the next.

"Maybe," Martha replied softly. "But I haven't been blessed with any more *kinner* on my doorstep recently."

Joshua turned his attention toward her and caught her smiling at him, her blue eyes shining. "I don't know if you'll ever be blessed like that again," he agreed. "Nor would you want to be. That adoption process, dealing with the *Englisch* lawyers, and all their government..."

Martha's smile blurred, but maintained. "I would do it again in a heartbeat," she replied. "Over and over again, in fact. I have no regrets, despite how long and difficult of a process it was."

Joshua's eyebrows raised with interest. "Would you really? Even after all the heartache and money you spent? Before you grew so attached to her."

Martha frowned, and Joshua realized how his question sounded. "I care for Elizabeth," he reminded her. "But they did not make the process easy on you or your *familye.* Your heart was so frail after losing Peter. I thought you were going to break throughout all that. I can't imagine that anyone would ever go through that process again."

His beautiful companion offered him a serene smile. "Elizabeth was put on my doorstep for a reason," she said simply. "*Gott* had a hand in it, and He will test us in many ways. It would not have been right if He had simply gifted me the child without any trials and tribulations. Nothing good ever comes to us without *warrick*. You know that as well as I do."

Unable to resist, Joshua reached up to cup Martha's face with his open palm. She gasped, taken aback by his sudden motion, but she did not pull away. "Your faith, your patience, all of you amazes me, Martha," he told her huskily. "I hope that one day, you will consider being my *weib*."

Visibly swallowing, Martha cupped her cheek closer to his hand, closing her eyes. "*Yah*, I think I could see myself being your *weib*, Josh," she replied quietly. His heart swelled with emotion, the words he had been yearning to hear for years finally reaching his ears.

"Really?" he choked. "I—do you think we can announce it in the fall?"

Martha nodded, holding his gaze. "I think so," she murmured. "I don't think there's anything else for us to learn about one another and I have no doubt that you are a *gut mann* and will be a good *vadder* to Elizabeth."

"You've made me so happy, Martha," he sputtered, cupping her other cheek and drawing her toward him for a long, sweet kiss.

"Is this your proposal, then?" she asked as they parted, her eyes darting nervously toward her daughter, who remained fixated on the ducklings.

Joshua dropped his hands and looked toward Elizabeth. He had almost forgotten the little girl was there in his excitement. Blushing, he laughed. "No. Let's call this...a discussion about our future," he offered. "But it's *gut* to know where we stand on the issue now."

She took his hand and squeezed it softly. "*Denki* for being so patient with me, Josh. I know it hasn't been easy, and you could have found someone else."

He shook his head vehemently, shocked that she could not see how much he cared about her. He was sure that his feelings were as clear as Brass Lake. "Even if I had to wait forever, Martha, there would never be anyone else for me. I thought I had been clear about that."

She cocked her head and lowered her eyelids bashfully. "I truly don't deserve you." She sighed. "But I am ready to move forward with you. These past weeks have shown me how lonely I've been."

He returned her hand squeeze and raised her fingers to his lips softly. "This time next year, we will be married," he promised, and Martha sat back happily against the blanket. Suddenly, Elizabeth ran up to them, a flock of ducks chasing her as she held up her cupped hands.

"Liza!" Martha gasped, sitting upright, her eyes popping as she realized what was going on. Joshua did not immediately realize what was happening. "What have you got in your hands?!"

The duckling squawked loudly, and Elizabeth chortled noisily, and he snapped into reality, understanding what their young charge had done. Joshua jumped up to rescue the baby before the mother duck could attack the child for taking off with her duckling.

"Elizabeth! You can't steal baby birds!" Martha whooped, shaking her head in mild panic.

"Give that to me," Joshua gasped with a laugh, freeing the crying babe from the child's confused hands.

"Why not?" Elizabeth demanded. "I want it!"

Only when the duckling was free did he exhale, scooping her

up and out of harm's way, but the mother duck was more concerned with her babe than she was with vengeance.

"I wanted to bring it *deheem*," Elizabeth complained, watching the birds return to the pond sadly.

"There are more than enough animals for you at home," Martha said primly, rising to gather their belongings. "Let's head back there before that mother duck brings her friends along for vengeance."

Chuckling, Joshua kept Elizabeth on his shoulders as he helped Martha collect the plates and containers which held the remnants of their picnic. Once they had packed everything away into the wicker basket, Martha neatly folded the checked blanket and they headed toward Joshua's brand new buggy.

They set Elizabeth in the back and sat together on the buckboard, checking on the girl through the glass window. She looked forlornly out the window toward the pond.

"Bye duckies," she mumbled sadly.

"Maybe I could build her a pond," Joshua suggested as they headed back toward the Hochstetler house, the gentle terrain bumping them along under the wheels of the buggy.

"You already spoil her enough as it is!" Martha laughed, but Joshua saw the look of appreciation she offered him.

"It's not spoiling when it's educational and beneficial for the *bauerie*," he countered. "Your *vadder* could make use of a fishing pond, couldn't he? You might even be able to sell some of the fish."

"But that's not why you'd do it," Martha replied, wagging her finger knowingly. "You'd do it so Elizabeth can play with the ducklings."

Joshua laughed again. "*Yah*, that is true," he admitted.

"It's not a bad idea," Martha continued slowly. "My *leit* will need more income when I leave the *haus*."

"Will you move into my *haus*? With my *familye*?" Joshua asked in surprised.

"Wouldn't I?"

"There are just so many of us living there already and your house is the only one that Elizabeth has ever known."

Silence fell between them, both of them contemplative.

"Would you like to move into my *haus*?" Joshua asked slowly, suddenly concerned.

"I just assumed that I would. It's how it's done if another house isn't being built."

"Sometime. We could build our own *haus*," Joshua offered, steering the buggy onto a solid road.

"That seems like a waste of resources," Martha offered sensibly. "We have two perfectly *gut* homes with families who care for us. *Yah*, it is true yours is more crowded than my *leit's*..."

She trailed off, considering it more.

"Martha, I am willing to do whatever you want to do," he reassured her.

"I know," she replied, flashing him a warm smile. "But we should do something that is feasible for everyone—including our families."

"We can discuss this more with them," Joshua said slowly. "After we've announced our intention to marry."

She met his eyes happily, nodding. "*Yah*. We can do that," she agreed.

They rode on for several minutes in silence, each lost in their own thoughts. Birdsong guided them over the backroads, where a random car or buggy would pass. Joshua waved at everyone impartially, his good mood floating him into the highest branches of the flourishing oak trees.

"Why are my *mudder* and *vadder* talking in loud voices?"

The shocking question dropped Joshua back to reality with a thud, his gaze falling on Martha's parents. In his happy daze, Joshua had barely noticed that he had ridden the entire way to the Hochstetler farm.

Esther and Amos dropped their animated arms the second they saw the trio returning, forcing pleasant looks on their face.

"*Hallo*!" Esther called out with far too much cheer. "How was the picnic?"

"I wanted a birdie, but they didn't let me take it *deheem*!" Elizabeth complained, freeing herself from the back of the buggy as soon as Jacob opened the door.

"That sounds like very smart advice," Amos told his granddaughter.

"Go inside and wash your hands, Eliza," Martha told her. The child skipped toward the door, and Martha followed up the steps with the basket in hand. She eyed her parents warily.

"What was going on when we arrived?" she asked.

"*Nix*," Amos said.

"You have mail," Esther piped in at the same time. Confusion overcame Joshua and he could see that Martha was equally perplexed.

"Mail?" she echoed, stepping forward.

"Estie, enough!" Amos frowned, his face twisting in a way that Joshua had never seen before. "She doesn't need to see it."

"Why wouldn't I need to see my own mail?" Martha demanded. "*Wat* is going on?"

"It's—"

"*Nix*!" Amos boomed, his voice rising so loudly the nearby chickens squeaked in protest. Both women fell silent.

"*Daed*, if I have mail, I would like to see it," Martha insisted. "Where is it? What kind of mail is it?"

"I said *nee*!" Amos cried. "I am still the *mann* of this *haus* and you will respect my decisions."

A heavy, pregnant pause fell between them as Martha's eyes bugged in shock. A hazy film covered her lovely irises. Joshua was certain she had never been spoken to in this way by her father before.

"Go inside and tend to you *dochder*," Amos ordered his own daughter. "She's been inside too long. Who knows what mischief she's gotten into?"

Without saying goodbye to Joshua, Martha hurried inside, the upset on her face palpable. Joshua gaped at the Hochstetlers, unsure of how to address this odd encounter.

"Is everything all right, Amos?" Joshua asked tentatively. "You're not acting like yourself."

"He needs to pray," Esther huffed, storming off to join her daughter and granddaughter in the house. The men stared at one another when they were alone, neither speaking.

"Is there something I can do?" Joshua offered awkwardly when the moment lingered too long. He wanted to excuse himself, but not without ensuring that everything was fine first. He could not begin to identify what was happening or why Amos was withholding information from his daughter. Amos regarded him for a long moment.

"What I am about to tell you is to be held in confidence," he warned. "You can't tell Martha."

Joshua hesitated. "I don't know if I feel comfortable with that—"

"It's a letter from the law firm in Cleveland," Amos blurted out. "The one that handled Elizabeth's adoption."

Joshua blinked slowly. "Why won't you give it to Martha then?" he asked worriedly.

"Why are they writing to her now?" Amos demanded. "Nothing *gut* can be in that letter."

A fusion of relief and exasperation twinged inside Joshua. "Maybe it's a follow-up, or they are providing her with more information. Don't you think she should see it and open it?"

Amos was unconvinced. "You sound like my *weib*," he complained. "I had hoped you would see it my way."

"What way is that, Amos?" Joshua was genuinely puzzled.

"You were there for the whole terrible process," Amos grumbled. "I thought we had put all that behind us. If she's going to keep receiving letters from that law firm, she'll never stop thinking of Elizabeth as that *bobbli* who was left on her doorstep instead of what she really is—a gift from *Gott*."

Joshua placed a comforting hand on the older man's shoulder. "I don't think you give Martha enough credit for her strength. She knows that Elizabeth is not just some *Englisch* baby left for her to raise. Elizabeth is one of us, a part of our community. The *bobbli* knows Martha is her *mudder*."

Amos eyed him begrudgingly. "You think I'm being a *fuhl?*"

"I think you are being a *gut vadder* and watching out for your only *kin* and *kinnskinn*," Joshua corrected him. "But Martha is a grown *frau* and Elizabeth is her *kin*. She has a right to know about anything that pertains to the *maedel*. You can't keep the letter from her, Amos, even to protect her."

The older man drew in a shaky breath and nodded, sinking down onto one of the wooden patio chairs. "You're right. I don't know what I was thinking."

"You were thinking about what's best for Elizabeth and Martha—as always."

"Will you call Martha out here, *pliese*?" Amos asked tiredly. "And have Esther bring the letter, too."

Nodding, Joshua retreated into the house, where he found the women chatting quietly in the kitchen. They jerked their heads up in unison when he entered, both their faces drawn with concern.

"He's ready to show you the letter, Martha," Joshua told her. Relief flooded her face, and she jumped up from the chair as Esther also stood. Her mother reached over the stove to retrieve the creamy envelope from its hiding spot among the spices and together, they headed toward Amos on the porch.

"*Es dutt mer leed*," Amos apologized, unable to look at his wife or daughter when they appeared in front of him.

Content that he had done everything he could to resolve the issue, Joshua turned to leave.

"Where are you going?" Martha called out plaintively.

He stopped and looked back, his brow furrowing. "This seemed like a *familye* affair..."

"Aren't you going to be a part of this *familye*?" she asked, sitting next to her father. Amos grinned lightly, stroking his salt and pepper beard nervously as Martha slid her finger along the flap of the formal-looking envelope.

Esther waved him forward and Joshua rejoined the Hochstetlers with their daughter. Serenely, Martha unfolded the thick page from within and began to read the typed letter to herself.

"What does it say?" Amos demanded. But Joshua did not need Martha to tell him something was terribly wrong. The air chilled as her expression froze, her beautiful eyes glassing over. She sat forward, her knuckles clenching against the paper as her lips gaped open.

"Martha?" Joshua demanded in alarm. "*Wat* is it?"

Her chin lifted and her eyes locked with Joshua's. Dread overcame him, his own breath catching as he tried to make sense of her expression.

I made a mistake! I shouldn't have told Amos to give her the letter!

But it was too late to go back now. Whatever the damage, it was done.

And for the first time in his life, Joshua watched in horror as Martha burst into tears.

CHAPTER 6

The words on the page made little sense to Martha, yet she understood them with far too much clarity simultaneously.

How can this be?

In the background, she heard her father, mother, and Joshua calling out to her, demanding an explanation, but she could not bring herself to formulate the words aloud. Silently, she handed the letter to her father, who grabbed it, scanning the typed print. Dizziness washed over her.

"T-this is nonsense!" he sputtered.

"What?" Joshua implored them, still uncomprehending.

"Where was this *mann* when the adoption was happening?" Amos fumed.

"May I?" Joshua asked, reaching for the letter when no one would explain the contents. Without a word of his own, Amos handed it to the young man, leaving only Esther in the dark. Elizabeth ran outside to join her family and Martha hastily wiped her eyes, rising from the chair. But her astute child had already caught the look of anguish on her mother's face and peered worriedly around the porch.

"I washed," she informed them, showing her hands. "See?"

Martha scooped her into a tight embrace, holding her close. "*Komme, liebling,*" she mumbled. "Let's get you ready for bed."

"It's too early!" Elizabeth complained, but Martha could not sit around thinking about the dreaded letter another moment.

"*Dienacht,* we sleep early," she insisted, carrying the child back into the house.

Despite Elizabeth's protests, the girl fell asleep in relatively short order once Martha had put her down. For a long while, she sat at the child's bedside, watching her small chest rise and fall, her heart pounding wildly in her ears.

"Martha."

The sound of her name being whispered from the doorway of Elizabeth's bedroom turned her around, and she found Joshua lingering against the jamb.

"Won't you *komme* back outside so we can discuss this?" he urged. "Your *leit* are very worried about that letter."

Swallowing, she rose and following him quickly downstairs, concerned that her daughter might overhear the words and somehow piece together the terrible situation unfolding.

Oh, how she wished she had not forced her father to let her see the correspondence now. How long had they been sitting on it? She had not bothered to look at the date, the shock of the information blocking everything else out.

Don't be narricht, she scolded herself. *Avoiding it won't make it go away.*

But what would?

Her parents huddled over the paper as she and Joshua regrouped outside. They almost did not seem to notice the younger people approach as they pored over each word.

"Could this be...what do the *Englisch* call those things... scams? I heard the Bontragers fell victim to one of those and lost a lot of money a few years ago—" Esther offered hopefully.

"It's not a scam, *Mamm,*" Martha said curtly, reclaiming the note to read again. She exhaled as she recognized that the letter was over two weeks old.

"How can you be sure? Why would this *mann* claim to have rights to Elizabeth now? After three years?" she insisted. "There was no mention of him in the adoption papers...was there?"

Her uncertainty only fueled Martha's worry.

Again, Martha reread the letter.

Dear Ms. Fischer,

I write to you regarding the matter of Elizabeth Fischer, aka Baby Girl Doe.

As the proposed legal mother of Elizabeth Fischer, it is my office's duty to inform you that a man has come forward disputing the adoption with a claim that he is the natural father of the child. I have no further information to pass along on this matter, but did feel it was my obligation to inform you of this immediately.

Although I cannot disclose any other information at this time, you are welcome to contact my office during regular business hours.

Respectfully Yours,

Angela Davis

Disbelievingly, Martha shook her head. "This tells me *nix*!" she exclaimed, upset. The fog had cleared from her eyes now. "I don't know *wu* this *mann* is or *wat* he wants! Is there going to be a court case? Will he take Elizabeth from me?"

"*Nee*!" all three of them chorused in unison.

"He can't," Joshua insisted. "The adoption is legal, binding."

"But if she's his *dochder*—"

"She is your *dochder*," Esther countered.

"You know what I mean, *Mamm*," Martha grumbled. "The *mann* must have some rights."

"Then he should have contested it when the adoption was happening," Amos interjected. "He can't change his mind now, after Elizabeth already has a *familye* who loves her. *Nee*. No one is taking our *maedel* away from us."

Suddenly, Martha found it difficult to breathe, her knees giving way as she sank into a chair. Joshua took her arm, guiding her down.

"It will be all right, *lieb*," he whispered, crouching down beside her. "*Gott* brought Eliza to us. He won't take her away."

He gave Peter to me too, Martha almost said, but held her tongue, averting her eyes from Joshua's kind, well-meaning stare. She did not have a good feeling about what was upcoming.

The last days of summer faded out, the heat lingering during the days, but the nights cooling some. Trees had yet to change, and usually Martha loved this time of year. Yet she could not bring herself to enjoy the excitement of the upcoming harvest months, not with the threat of a strange man looking for Elizabeth out there.

Her call to the lawyer had proven as useless as the letter. Like the note, it provided no additional information, but she had anticipated as much.

"There is nothing we can do but wait for him to make his next move," Angela Davis explained.

"And if he does? Then what?" Martha demanded.

"We'll cross that bridge when we come to it," she offered unhelpfully.

There was no word on this mystery man or his intentions after that letter, and Martha did her best to go about her days as if it had never happened.

She worked the farm with her parents, tending to her rambunctious little daughter. But every night, she prayed harder than she ever had before, begging God that he keep her happy life intact.

Joshua noticed the strain of the threat and did his best to comfort her.

"Surely if the man was serious, we would have heard something by now," he offered in his usual, optimistic way as they returned home from a buggy ride one evening. His hand reached for hers, and she begrudgingly allowed him to take it, even though she did not feel very affectionate. "Maybe your parents were right all along. It was someone's idea of a cruel joke."

The idea did not make Martha feel any better.

"What kind of person toys with another's emotions like that?" she demanded, angry at the notion. "I can't sleep, imagining the worst."

Joshua made a commiserating sound and squeezed her hand gently. "Eliza is safe and so are you," he promised. "In fact—"

The words died on his lips as he steered the buggy up the gravel driveway toward the Hochstetler's porch. Martha stiffened as she rested her eyes on the shiny, expensive car parked in front of the house.

"Are you expecting someone?" Joshua asked lightly, but she caught the concern in his tone. Panic flooded her heart and without waiting for the buggy to fully stop, she leaped off the buckboard, rushing toward the entranceway.

Loud voices met her ears before she saw anyone.

"...don't give a rat's behind! I want to see my daughter!" the stranger's growly voice commanded. "I didn't drive all the way into this hick town to leave empty-handed!"

Martha burst through the front door, her heart in her throat as she took in the scene in the front room.

A huge, well-dressed man in a cowboy hat and bolo tie whirled around to narrow his icy green eyes at Martha. Her parents cowered worriedly by the sofa, both standing, but clearly alarmed.

"Great! Another member of *Little House on the Prairie*. Who is raising my kid anyway?" he yelled. "Kid? Where are you?"

He stomped toward the entranceway, his boots tracking mud along the pristine wooden floors. Everything about him was offensive and loud. His tone reverberated through the peaceful living room and Martha's well-honed ears caught Elizabeth's soft whimpering from the second floor. Like her parents, Martha found herself paralyzed and unable to react.

Her worst nightmare was coming to fruition.

"I want my kid!" he boomed, his eyes boring into Martha's. "Where is she? You can't keep her from me! She's mine."

"I am going to have to ask you to leave, sir." Martha had not realized Joshua had followed in behind her, his tone even and clipped as he stood confidently behind her. Trembling, Martha looked back, but through her peripheral vision, she caught a flurry of movement on the stairs.

Elizabeth!

"Who the heck are you?" the man snorted.

"You are in the Hochstetler's house, sir. I think you are the one who should be making introductions, not demands," Joshua countered, without stuttering. Martha stepped protectively toward her daughter, hoping to shield her before the man could see her.

"The name's Rex Matheson, and that kid y'all've been raising is mine. Bring her to me."

"Mamm?"

Martha could not breathe now, her knees knocking as she put herself between Rex Matheson and the child. The sneering man's face lit up into the ugliest smile. "Ah. There you are."

His lips curled upward, and he extended a hand toward her to touch her face. Instantly, Elizabeth recoiled and burst into tears.

"Don't be a brat!" he snapped, annoyance fully taking over his expression. "I'm your father. Come and let me take a look at you."

"*Nee*!" Elizabeth yelled, backing away.

Grimacing, Rex eyed them with disgust. "You really did a number on her, didn't you? She even speaks funny."

"You're not welcome here, Mr. Matheson," Joshua told him coldly. "And you're upsetting Elizabeth. Please leave or I'll have to contact the authorities."

"Go ahead!" Rex taunted. "I'll tell them how you kidnapped my daughter!"

Shaking violently now, Martha glanced from Joshua to her parents, who had gone deathly pale at the threat.

"There is a legal adoption in place, Mr. Matheson. You should have contested it when you first abandoned your child, three years ago."

Rex Matheson's face turned so dark, Martha was genuinely afraid. "You dumb-dumb," he spat. "If I'd know about the little brat, you think I'd let her be raised by a bunch of backward yokels?"

But he did not attempt to touch the sobbing child again. Instead, he threw his hands up and stalked toward the door, tracking more mud as he moved. "You ain't heard the last of me. Look me up. I'm Rex Matheson. I got more money than God, and I'll do whatever it takes to keep what's mine. You mark my words. That kid is coming home with me, eventually."

Without waiting for anyone to respond, he banged his way out the door, allowing it to slam behind him.

"Shh, it's all right, *liebling*," Martha told her daughter, cuddling her close as her parents finally regained their movements.

"Why did you let him in here?" Martha cried.

"He said he wanted to speak with us. We thought it was business, not about Eliza!" Amos protested.

"This isn't their fault," Joshua intervened smoothly. "And no harm was done."

Martha scoffed lightly, nodding at her wailing daughter. "No harm?!" she repeated. "He's done too much harm already, and he hasn't even started yet!"

Joshua put a strong hand on her shoulder, but Martha shrugged it off. No amount of words of pretend comfort were going to make any of this better.

CHAPTER 7

Under Joshua's urging, Martha called Angela Davis back again, but was unable to reach the lawyer at her office.

"I'll be sure to give Ms. Davis your message, Ms. Fischer," the law clerk promised. "But she's in court all day today."

"It's very urgent," Martha begged from the community phone at the King's store. She looked around nervously, worried that she might be overheard. "Please have her call this number and wait for me to respond. I will call her back right away."

"I'll let her know," came the response.

The call did not leave Martha feeling any more hopeful as she hung up and joined Joshua and Elizabeth on his buggy outside. Storm clouds swept in from the north, gathering over Sugar Lake to match Martha's darkening mood. Ever since Rex Matheson's arrival, the weather had been bad, as if God were mimicking her innermost thoughts.

For the past three days, she had been on tenterhooks, expecting the man to march back in and take her daughter from her arms. And if Rex were to do exactly that, what would they be able to do to stop him? Did he have any legal standing as Elizabeth's father? Was he really Elizabeth's father?

"*Mamm, eepie?*" Elizabeth called from her spot by the buggy, pointing toward the nearby bakery, across from the King's store. Martha almost refused, her desire to take her daughter home and hide too overwhelming. But Joshua nodded, taking the girl by the hand to lead the way across the road. Martha had little choice but to follow along.

Inside the store, wafts of cinnamon and sugar filled Martha's nose. Usually, the comforting smells would revert her back to pleasant childhood memories, the pretty shapes behind the display cases catching her attention.

Today, all she could think about was getting home.

"Did you speak to the *loiyer?*" Joshua asked as Elizabeth peered at the glass, oohing and ahhing at the various designs.

"Can I have two *eepies?*" she begged.

"*Nee,*" Martha interjected before Joshua could indulge her. "One is enough. And you'll get one for *Mammi* too."

"And *Daddi?*" Elizabeth suggested.

"All right," Martha relented, relaxing slightly at her daughter's giving personality. "One for *Daddi* too."

"And Josh?"

"*Nee.*" Joshua laughed. "I don't need cookies."

"Nor do I before you ask," Martha added, sensing her next question. Elizabeth grinned impishly, and Martha exhaled. She turned her attention back to Joshua and shook her head. "*Nee*. She's in court all day. I don't know if I will hear back from her."

"She did try to warn us," he offered.

"Warn us about what, though?" Martha complained. "She only said that we would deal with this issue if it arose. Now that it's arisen, she's nowhere to be found."

Joshua leaned against the wall as the proprietor walked out of the back, wiping her hands on her apron. "*Guten nammidaag*!" she called pleasantly. "Eliza, look how much you've grown!"

"I'm going to be tall, like my *Mamm*," Elizabeth told the owner proudly, and she cast Martha a knowing smile.

"*Yah*, and just as kind and beautiful, too," the baker agreed. "What kind of *eepie* would like today?"

The woman and Elizabeth bantered back and forth as Joshua and Martha resumed their conversation.

"How can he believe he is her father when we don't even know who the *mudder* is?" Joshua mused, echoing Martha's own thoughts. "How did he find Angela Davis? What made him seek her out?"

In all the stress of what had happened, Martha admitted she had never considered that question before. She knew very little about Elizabeth's biological mother or father, but she had always assumed Angela Davis and the government had known their details. Could everyone have been in the dark about them?

"Could it be a case of mistaken identity?" Joshua suggested and Martha felt a smidgen of hope.

"There are ways to determine that, aren't there?" she asked, but their conversation was cut short as Joshua was summoned forward to pay for Elizabeth's treats.

All the way back to the house, Martha weighed the notion of a mistaken identity case. Perhaps Rex Matheson was just a man looking for his lost child. She could extend him some grace—provided he left her child alone.

At the same time, she hoped she never had to see the bloated and pompous Mr. Matheson again. His arrogance had left a foul taste in her mouth.

Esther was working in the garden when they arrived home. Elizabeth darted up to her grandmother, handing her a paper bag with a cookie.

"Is this for me, *liebling*," Esther cooed. "*Denki*!"

Joshua turned to Martha. "I should get back to my *familye*," he said regretfully. "Will you let me know if the *loiyer* calls?"

Martha nodded, offering him a weak smile. "I will, Josh. We'll see you on *Sunndaag, yah*? For *karrich*?"

He bobbed his head and Martha's heart tightened with regret.

Poor Joshua. He's always taking care of me, of us. When will it just be our time? Or is this Gott's way of saying it's not meant for it to be our time, ever?

Pushing the thought out of her head, she waved him goodbye as he climbed back onto his buggy and disappeared out of sight, leaving the females alone in the garden to pick fresh vegetables for dinner.

Amos eventually returned from his work with the animals and collected his granddaughter, the pair racing around the house in one of their silly games.

Martha did not hear the car until it was almost beside the garden, an old muffler sputtering and coughing out gray smoke amongst the fresh herbs and vegetables.

Dread encompassed Martha, her head jerking to the vehicle. "Take Eliza into the house!" she called to her mother, racing toward the vehicle.

But as she neared, she instantly realized that it was not Rex Matheson driving.

A fair, freckled face girl of no more than twenty peered out of the rolled-down window, her hazel eyes blinking warily around the landscape. Her gaze landed on Martha, her mouth forming an "O" of surprise.

Martha's chest tightened, her pulse erratic as she stared at the young woman, something hauntingly familiar about her face.

"Martha Fischer?" she asked quietly, turning off the choking vehicle.

"Who are you?" Martha demanded, her voice shaking.

"My name is Joanna...Laurence. Can I talk with you for a minute? I promise I won't take up much of your time."

She started to get out of the car, but Martha held up a hand to stop her. "Did Rex Matheson send you?" she challenged. "If so, you're not welcome here!"

Joanna's face paled. "Oh...no," she whispered. "Has he been here already?"

Confusion flooded Martha as she studied the young woman's face, trying to understand what she wanted.

"Please, I just…I—"

"Who are you?" Martha asked again. "What do you want?"

"I'm…" she paused and took a deep breath. "I'm the girl who left my baby on your doorstep three years ago."

Amos took Elizabeth into town and Esther made coffee. It was plain to see why Martha had been so drawn to the flame-haired woman at first. The resemblance to her daughter was uncanny now that Joanna had identified herself.

"I-I'm very sorry to pop in on you like this," Joanna apologized for what seemed like the tenth time since she had stepped foot on the property. She was such a stunning contrast to the boisterous, obnoxious man who had stomped through the Hochstetler home with dirty boots, trying to stake his claim. "I want you to know I'm not here to upset your life in any way whatsoever."

Martha wanted to believe her, the wide, amber green of her eyes guileless and worried, but if that were true, what was Joanna doing here so soon after Rex Matheson?

"Why did you come?" Esther asked gently, sitting in her favorite chair. Joanna took another quivering breath and bit on her lower lip, clutching her coffee mug with both hands.

"I came to warn you about Rex," she confessed in a rush of breath. "That he might come here."

Dubiously, Martha eyed her mother across the room, but Esther remained fixed on the woman, as if she were trying to understand Joanna's mentality.

"I think you best start from the beginning," Esther suggested kindly, and Joanna did.

She lifted her light auburn head and met Martha's eyes sadly, setting her cup down without taking a sip. "When I was sixteen, I ran away from home," she admitted. "My family was not…very nice. I'll spare you the details."

Martha's heart twinged for her as she wrung her hands nervously in anticipation. "I made my way to Ohio and onto one of the Matheson ranches. He has a bunch of them—you might not know his name, but he's huge in the beef business."

"He certainly thinks a lot of himself," Martha commented, and Joanna chuckled mirthlessly.

"I admit, I was taken with him…at first," she confessed, sounding embarrassed. "I had no family, no money, and he seemed so much larger than life…"

"Oh…" Martha gasped. "He really is her father!"

Joanna darted her eyes down. "He is not fit to be anyone's father," she murmured. "That's why I ran off as soon as I found out I was pregnant. I knew I couldn't raise the baby alone and when I saw you, Martha…"

The young widow sat up straighter, blinking. "You saw me?" she repeated. "When?"

"I came to Sugar Lake to hide," Joanna whispered. "I spent time in one of the rented cottages throughout the last part of my pregnancy, ordering in most of the time. But sometimes,

I would take walks and see you. You always looked so sad, so lost. I wanted to make you smile."

Tears brimmed at the edges of Martha's eyes. "You don't know me," she whispered. "How could you tell that?"

Joanna shrugged. "Maybe one lost soul to another? I don't know. All I knew was that I couldn't raise the baby on my own. I was a seventeen-year-old kid with no job and an abusive boss and baby daddy. I had to protect her. This was the last place anyone would think to look for her, if Rex ever found out about her."

Martha swallowed the lump in her throat, thinking of all the turmoil and heartache this girl had already endured in her young life.

"You went back to him after Elizabeth was born?"

Joanna's mouth twitched at the corners, her eyes shining. "No," she replied. "I didn't."

"You must have," Esther insisted, her wise eyes narrowing. "How else did he find out about the baby and the lawyer?"

"That was my own stupidity." Joanna sighed. "I've been emailing and texting with one of the other stable hands since I left. Either he told Rex or Rex saw the messages. Either way, he learned the truth and hunted me down in Cleveland, where I was staying. He beat me within an inch of my life before I gave him the lawyer's name."

Martha gasped, horrified. "Have you gone to the authorities?" she demanded, sickened to think that the man had been in her house.

Joanna laughed hollowly, shaking her head. "No. They don't do anything to men like Rex Matheson. He's too rich. But that was the last time he was going to lay a hand on me. I won't let him anywhere near Elizabeth."

"What choice do we have if he's her father?" Martha asked worriedly. "He might just do what he says."

"I won't let him," Joanna insisted. "I signed off on that adoption with Angela Davis. It's legal and binding. I was sure of it when I did the paperwork."

Nervously, Martha twisted her fingers. "But if he's as powerful and wealthy as you say…"

"I'm staying in Sugar Lake for now," Joanna explained. "Back at the same cottage as when I was pregnant with Elizabeth. I won't get in your way, but I will be nearby if you need me."

"That doesn't sound safe, *liebling*," Esther said worriedly. "What if he sees you?"

"I can take care of myself," Joanna promised. "You take care of Elizabeth. Please?"

Martha and Esther exchanged nervous looks, their fear palpable as Joanna rose. "I didn't mean to cause you any stress. I only ever wanted Elizabeth safe. If he gets her hands on her now, he'll only treat her like a piece of cattle. The only reason he wants her is for a prize, or to show he can. It's not paternal. It's just one more thing to add to Rex Matheson's collection of stuff. Don't let Elizabeth become one of his trinkets."

"We will keep her safe," Martha vowed. "Rex Matheson won't put one hand on her."

Joanna smiled warmly at Martha. "I know. You have something about you, Martha, something…I don't know. But I felt at peace when I saw you all those years ago. She's in good hands here. This is what a family is supposed to feel like."

Martha walked her toward the door, pity for the life-beaten soul breaking her heart. "Are you sure you're safe there, at the cottage? You could stay here with us..."

"Martha!" Esther chided her scoldingly, but Martha was not surprised when Joanna shook her head vehemently.

"I don't need anything from you, Martha. You have already given me the greatest gift there is—security for Elizabeth." She paused at the threshold. "It will only confuse the girl if I'm here...and honestly, it would be hard for me to see her, too."

Joanna smiled wanly. "Elizabeth was my aunt's name, by the way—my mom's sister. She was the only person in my family who ever cared about me. I'm glad you named the baby Elizabeth."

The three mothers shared a powerful gaze, and Joanna turned to leave. "I will come around and check in. I'm aware you don't have phones, so I'll do my best to come when I don't see Elizabeth." She hesitated. "If that's okay. Just until this is resolved. I don't want to overstep, but I won't be able to rest until I know he's out of her life for good."

Martha wondered if Joanna was asking for the moon.

"You're welcome here anytime," she reassured the young woman. "You don't have to avoid Elizabeth."

"It's better for me if I do." Joanna said quickly.

"We'll pray for you," Esther promised.

"Thanks," Joanna sighed, turning away. "I think we're all going to need a bit of God's grace to see us through this."

CHAPTER 8

Joshua gaped at the women, shaking his head in disbelief. "You just allowed her in for *kaffe*? After what happened with Rex Matheson?" he demanded in disbelief.

"You'll understand when you meet her," Martha insisted, frowning slightly. "She's *nix* like that *mann*."

"She's not," Esther agreed, taking a crate of supplies from the back of the buggy as they continued to unload from their trip into town. "And she looks so much like a grown version of Elizabeth."

Joshua eyed the women suspiciously, wondering if perhaps they were losing their sense of good judgement. "What did Amos have to say about this?"

"Amos took Elizabeth away," Esther explained. "He hasn't met her yet. But she will be back. You'll both meet her."

Joshua had a peculiar sensation in his gut, unsure if he liked all these English newcomers popping into their quiet, peaceful lives. Things had been so much simpler before Rex

Matheson came along. He missed the days of only vying for Martha's love.

The little time he spent alone with Martha these days, their conversation was understandably dominated with talk of Elizabeth and Rex Matheson's next move. Joshua felt as though he could foresee the future and he did not like what he saw.

"Has Angela Davis called back yet?" he asked.

"*Nee.*" Martha sighed. "But Joanna seems convinced that the adoption is unbreakable."

She sounded nervous and unconvinced. Joshua did not blame her. No one in their community knew enough about legal standing to honestly comment on this.

"Oh no!"

Amos' voice called out from the porch and all heads whipped toward the road where a shiny pickup truck raced too fast up their driveway.

"Take Eliza!" Martha yelled, waving him back. Joshua slammed the back of his buggy closed and darted toward the front of the driveway to intercept the latest visitors, Esther and Martha, at his side.

"I will handle this, Martha," he told her in a low voice as Rex Matheson's smug face came into view. But he was not alone, the overdressed man driving, pushing open the driver's side door and allowing himself out with an attaché case in hand.

"Who is Martha Fischer?" he demanded. "I want to speak with Martha Fischer!"

His voice was abnormally loud, and he sniffed the air as if it smelled foul, squinting through his wire-framed glasses at the trio as Rex slowly ambled out of his spot. The arrogant rancher leaned cockily against the truck and folded his arms, tipping his Stetson hat back to watch.

"Hello?" the whiny, loud-mouth man called out. "Martha Fischer? This is the Fischer farm, isn't it?"

"No," Joshua corrected him. "It's not."

The answer brought his smugness down a notch, the rancher also losing his smirk.

The man with the briefcase stepped forward, thrusting a business card toward Joshua, who barely acknowledged it. He already sensed it was a lawyer without reading the fine print.

"Mark Hanlon. I represent Mr. Matheson's interests. I'm here to claim his daughter, one minor child, three years old?"

Joshua glanced back at Martha. Her complexion had gone opaque, but before he could speak, another vehicle started up the driveway in a cloud of black smoke. This one sputtered along, chugging unhealthily. Martha gasped beside him. "It's Joanna," she rasped.

"You will not be claiming any child," Joshua replied shortly, ignoring the car approaching and facing the lawyer, whose attention was now split between his client and the approaching car. The young woman stopped and got out of her vehicle.

"Joanna?" Rex snarled, pushing himself off the truck. "What the devil are you doing here?"

"I could ask you the same thing, Rex," she retorted. "Don't you have better things to do than bother honest people?"

Rex guffawed loudly, but Joshua could see there was not a hint of mirth in his cold, verdant eyes as he glowered at the young woman. "There ain't a dang honest thing about what happened here. I want what's mine and I ain't leaving until I get it!"

Joshua's pulse quickened as he sensed danger, an electrical current charging between them. He was not the only one to feel trouble and Mark Hanlon put himself between the burly man and slender, nervous girl.

"You have no standing to withhold a child from her biological father," the lawyer intoned, fixing his eyes on Joshua as if he assumed he were Martha's husband. "You have twenty-four hours to relinquish custody of the child in question or you will find yourself on the side of a civil suit the likes of which this town will never recover from. I will sue for emotional damages, pain and suffering..."

He launched into a legal diatribe which Joshua did not attempt to understand, his eyes growing wider and wider with each word. In the interim, Rex's grin grew larger, as if he'd just swallowed a whole canary.

"You can't just take a child from the only family she's ever known!" Martha cried out in anguish. "Think of what that will do to Elizabeth!"

"Elizabeth," Rex drawled slowly and Joshua realized he was hearing the name for the first time.

"You didn't even know her name!" he scoffed furiously. "What do you want with her?"

"She's mine!" Rex spat. "I take what's mine, and that's that!"

"You have one day to get your affairs in order. Then we'll be back for the child," the lawyer informed them. "Come along, Rex."

"I ain't done here," he said, ambling closer to Joanna. The young woman flinched and backed away, clearly afraid of the man. Before he could stop himself, Joshua placed himself firmly in the man's face.

"Whatever right you think you have to the child, you have no standing on this land," Joshua told him firmly. "You are trespassing on private property."

Rex leered at Joshua, but a look of uncertainty passed his face when Joanna piped in, "There's a 'Stand Your Ground' law in Ohio, isn't there, Mr. Hanlon?"

Joshua did not understand what any of that meant. Yet Joanna's words wiped the arrogance off Rex's face. "Don't be stupid," he grumbled. "They're pacifists."

"We've said our piece, Rex. Let's go," Mark Hanlon offered, sounding vaguely nervous himself, and the men started back toward the shiny pickup truck, casting Joshua a sideways glance as if they thought he might attack.

"Twenty-four hours or you'll be dealing with the courts. And I know how much you folks love dealing with our laws." Mark chuckled coldly out the window.

Joshua only exhaled when they drove off, leaving them all in a blanket of dust from the gravel. Esther waved her hand over her face and coughed, and Joshua spun around to look after Martha. Tears pooled in her luminous eyes, and she dropped to her knees. Joanna placed a comforting hand on her shoulder.

"I'm so sorry," the young woman whispered, the guilt in her face palpable. "I should have never told him anything..."

"This is not your fault," Esther cut in quickly. "That *mann's* decisions are not on your shoulders, Joanna."

Silence fell as Joanna lifted her head to look at Joshua. "Hi," she offered weakly. "I'm—"

"I know who you are," he told her tiredly. "I am Joshua Troyer. Martha's…"

He trailed off, unsure of how to finish the sentence. Their whole future had been put on hold.

"Are they gone?" Amos called out from the porch, his eyes darting around the yard.

"*Yah, Daed,*" Martha replied, rising to wipe her eyes. "But they will be back. They won't stop until they take Elizabeth."

"*Mamm*!" Elizabeth sprinted out of the house as Amos tried to catch her. The little girl was too quick and jutted toward Martha. Joshua saw Joanna balk and gasp, taking a step back as she stared at the tiny replica of herself.

Martha scooped the child into her arms and held her against her chest, smothering the urge to cry.

"What's the matter, *Mamm*?" Elizabeth cooed, peering curiously at Joanna. Their identical hazel eyes locked on one another and Joanna's gaze bugged as if she realized just how much the child resembled her.

"*Hallo*!" Elizabeth called sweetly. "Are you *freind* with my *mamm*?"

"I-I have to go," Joanna stammered, backing away.

"Joanna—" Martha started to say, but the younger girl shook her head vehemently.

"No, I'm sorry. I-I will be back. We won't let him win, Martha. I promise…" Her voice cracked as she hurried away. No one stopped her as she climbed into her rusted vehicle and disappeared down the roadway, leaving the family alone and staring after her worriedly.

The moment Joanna disappeared in a cloud of black smoke, the skies opened up overhead and fat drops of rain began to pelt over them in a torrent.

"*Komme*, let's get inside," Esther told everyone, waving them toward the porch. But Joshua found himself oddly frozen in place, unable to move as he considered the predicament they found themselves facing.

In twenty-four hours, Elizabeth might be gone from their lives forever. Martha had barely recovered from Peter's death. She would certainly never recover from the loss of her daughter.

"Josh!" Martha called from the veranda. He turned to look at her, her face twisted in sorrow already, as if she knew what was upcoming. They could not take on a man like Rex Matheson. They did not have the resources or legal knowledge.

Nausea gripped his gut at the thought of losing the little girl he had helped raise since infancy.

There had to be a way to keep her in the district where she belonged.

With Martha, the only mother she had ever known.

CHAPTER 9

Little was said as the rain pounded against the house. Martha and Esther busied themselves in the kitchen preparing supper. Everyone was lost in thought, even as the men entertained the little girl with games, trying to take their own minds off the trouble brewing as intensely around them as the storm.

"*Mamm*, I'm scared!" Elizabeth cried when the thunder rumbled, appearing to shake the walls slightly. The words brought a fresh round of tears to Martha's eyes.

"You have *nix* to be afraid of, *liebling*," Martha told her daughter tenderly as she struggled against her emotions. "*Gott* knows the trees and grass need *wasser*. He is blessing the earth as He blesses us."

"I'm going to pray for the thunder and rain to *schtop*," Elizabeth insisted. "I don't like it."

Wiping her hands on her apron, Martha took the child's hands and led her back to the living room where her father and Joshua sat.

"Why don't we all pray?" she suggested quietly. "I think we could all use *Gott*'s guidance right now."

Thunder rumbled outside again, and Elizabeth snuggled closer to her mother as she lowered herself to her knees. Amos and Joshua bowed their heads, Elizabeth and Martha following suit. Behind her eyelids, Martha struggled not to cry.

Pliese, Gott, don't take my darling daughter away. She is happy here, loved. That mann will not care for her the way we will. We only want what's best for her—

A loud pounding on the front door caused everyone to squeak in unison. Joshua jumped up as Martha put a protective hand out to keep her daughter back.

"Who's there?" Joshua called out without opening the door.

"It's Hannah King!" the woman screeched. "There's a call for Martha at the store."

Joshua threw open the door and stared at the store owner's eldest daughter, drenched from the rain.

"Oh Hannah!" Martha cried, rushing toward her. "You're soaked!"

"My father said you were waiting on an important call," Hannah explained, entering with a shiver. "He insisted that I run over here and tell you about it right away."

"Go fetch her a towel, Eliza," Martha urged her daughter. "Joshua will drive us both back to the store."

Joshua nodded in agreement as he glanced toward Amos. "Can I take your buggy? I'd rather not run *deheem* for mine."

Amos snorted. "You don't need to ask," he replied. "Take them."

Elizabeth toddled back with a fresh cloth for Hannah and, when she was dry, the three headed into the rainstorm toward the King's store and the community phone.

"Angela Davis said she would wait for your call as long as she could," Hannah recited from the buckboard as they slipped and slid through the mud, the gentle beating of rain timing their ride rhythmically.

Warily, Martha glanced at Joshua.

Was it a coincidence that Hannah had appeared just when they had been praying for an answer?

She did not dare hope. Martha had been disappointed before.

Dawn brought the most beautiful sunrise Martha had ever seen. The storm had raged for most of the night, but the early morning allowed for sunshine to glint off the slowly changing trees. Droplets of water remained on the leaves, painting the flowers in a prism of colors.

Yet Martha could not appreciate a single moment of it. Anxiety gnawed at the base of her stomach, the past week weighing on her like a leaden balloon.

"Did you sleep at all?"

Her mother's voice coaxed Martha back to the present, and she glanced back as her mother handed her a cup of coffee. The thought of putting anything in her system made Martha's stomach flip, but she took the cup anyway, only to appease her mother.

"*Nee*," she admitted. "I'm too nervous about today."

"Me too," Esther confessed. "Your *vadder* slept like a log, though."

A smile twitched at the corners of her mouth. "So did Elizabeth." She sighed. "She doesn't know about any of this."

"There's no need to tell her," Esther insisted.

"There is if she's going to be taken away," Martha cried, confusion overwhelming her again.

"She—"

The sound of a car approaching ended their conversation abruptly, and Martha stood, steeling her nerves. The sleek, black sedan stopped and a handsome, stately woman exited the driver's seat, a taut smile on her face.

"Forgive the earliness of this meeting," Angela Davis informed her apologetically. "But really, it's the only time I have all day."

"I would rather get this over and done with," Martha said honestly.

"I appreciate that," Angela stated softly. "Frankly, it's ridiculous that it's even come to this."

"I agree," Esther grunted, nodding approvingly at the woman. "You're sure—"

The crunching of gravel distracted her again as Joshua hurried up the driveway. His brow creased when he saw Angela.

"Who is this?" he demanded, his emotions on high alert.

"Angela, Joshua," Martha explained, but before proper introductions could commence, the sputtering of Joanna's old car and headlights of Mark Hanlon's shiny truck all came into view.

Martha's neck was so stiff, she was sure it might snap with one wrong movement.

"Everyone is here," Martha muttered, stepping back, her hand at her chest.

"You let me handle this," Angela warned the group, her eyes settling on Joanna as she climbed out of the car. "Joanna Laurence?"

"You're Angela. I remember you!" the young woman croaked. "You're the one who handled the adoption paperwork."

"Yes," Angela conceded as Mark Hanlon and his client exited their overstated truck.

"What the heck is all this?" Rex spat. "A party? I was told I was getting my kid this morning!"

"No, Mr. Matheson," Angela replied, spinning around. "You were told that we were going to resolve this issue. I am Angela Davis. I handled the adoption for Elizabeth Fischer."

"Matheson," Rex fired back. "She's a Matheson."

Angela nodded and stomped forward. "Are you willing to submit to a DNA test to confirm your paternity?"

Rex glowered at her as Martha tried to catch her breath. Joshua slipped up the stairs, joining her side to hold her up as if he could see how weak she was getting as the scene unfolded.

"Is the little witch suggesting the kid ain't mine now?" Rex guffawed. "Yeah, I'll submit to a DNA test."

Joanna hung her head. Martha closed her eyes, praying harder than she ever had before.

"To be clear, Mr. Matheson," Angela drawled, ambling closer to him, unbothered by his smugness. "If you are found to be that child's father, it will be proof that you engaged in certain activities with a sixteen-year-old girl."

Martha's eyes popped open in time to watch the smirk on both Rex's face and his lawyer's freeze.

"The age of consent is sixteen in Ohio," Mark choked out. His words only deepened the scowl on his client's mouth.

"Be that as it may," Angela agreed. "I wonder how that will play out with the public. I imagine your shareholders and board will have some...questions for you. And likely your ex-wife, too. Weren't you married when this affair began? I wonder if the divorce agreement might be altered when this comes to light."

Rex took a deep, shuddering breath as the sun fully broke over the horizon, basking the entire landscape in light.

"W-what do you want?" the rancher stuttered.

"No, what? Rex, we'll fight this—" his lawyer started.

"Shut it, Mark!" Rex barked. "Give them what they want!"

"You will need to sign away your parental rights and any further claim to the child, here and now," Angela told him.

"This sounds a lot like extortion," Mark whined.

"I am laying out the facts for you, Mr. Hanlon. Your client, although despicable, has not broken any laws that I can prove here and now. He can choose to do whatever he pleases. But know this; should he choose to go after custody, the Hochstetlers, Ms. Fischer and the entire district are willing to put down all their resources to fight him. Nothing will stay unaired, so I hope he likes his dirty laundry fresh on the line."

Rex was opaque as he stared at his lawyer.

"I haven't got all day, gentlemen," Angela yelled. "What's the verdict?"

"Send the paperwork to my office," Rex rasped, storming back toward the truck. His lawyer rushed to follow him and they were gone before anyone could blink.

"*Wat* just happened?" Joshua whispered as Martha shrugged, looking to the attorney for clarification.

Joanna threw her arms around Angela, and the lawyer grimaced. "You were amazing!" the young woman squealed. "I never thought about exposing him to our relationship!"

Angela looked at her sadly. "You should have reported him when he put his hands on you, honey," she said and sighed.

"It's not too late, is it?" Martha offered, stepping forward.

"No…," Angela agreed. "But it will be a long process to get justice."

Joanna shook her auburn head and exhaled shakily. "No. I just want to put Ohio and Rex Matheson behind me for good," she said. "It's the only way I'm going to move forward."

"I'll keep you all updated on the paperwork," Angela promised. "But I don't think you need to worry about Rex Matheson coming around anymore."

Hurrying down the steps, Martha stood in front of the lawyer and her daughter's mother. "I-I don't know how to thank you both," she breathed. "If you weren't here…"

"I wouldn't be doing my job if I wasn't here putting that man in his place," Angela replied. "And on that note, I do have to get going. Talk to you soon."

She disappeared into her car and they waved her off. Martha smiled weakly at Joanna. "Will you come in for breakfast at least?" she offered.

Joanna shook her head, glancing back at Martha's parents and Joshua. "I meant what I said about getting out of Ohio. I told you I was only sticking around to make sure Elizabeth was safe."

"Thank you, Joanna."

"The only thanks I need is one you've already given me. You've given my baby girl something I couldn't— security."

The women embraced and Joanna sniffled, stepping back as Elizabeth darted onto the front porch.

"Mamm?"

"I should go," Joanna whispered.

"Wait…" Martha begged, extending her hand back toward the little girl. "If you want…?"

Joanna pursed her lips and stared sadly at Elizabeth before nodding slowly. "All right."

"Komme, liebling. Meet *Mamm's freind."*

Elizabeth skipped down the steps in her nightgown. Her face lit up in a pleased smile, glad to meet a new friend.

Joshua rejoined Martha's side, his hand finding hers as Joanna crouched down to meet her child face to face for the first time in years.

"You are a *gut frau,* Martha Fischer," Joshua whispered.

"I must have learned from a *gut mann,* Joshua Troyer," she murmured back. "Now, what were we doing before we were so rudely interrupted? Ah *yah.* Making plans to announce our betrothal, weren't we?"

EPILOGUE

Puffs of white escaped the children's mouths as they ran through the snow, tripping over their thick woolen clothes.

"Be careful!" Martha called out to Elizabeth with a laugh, but the little girl was already plowing headlong into a snowman, her friends following.

"This is why we don't get married in the dead of winter," Esther chided her. Martha's eyes traveled across the crowded, snow-capped lawn toward her groom amongst the many guests. Despite the freezing outdoor venue, everyone appeared to be having a good enough time, the younger children and feeding mothers tucked away in the house and heated barn where they could be warmed by the fires and woodstoves.

"We didn't want to wait until spring," Martha reminded her mother, locking eyes with her groom.

"Isn't that something?" Esther teased. "A year ago, you couldn't even commit to going on a date with the *mann* and suddenly, you could not wait to marry him."

But it was not a shock, not really. After all, they had been through together, between Peter and Elizabeth's adoption, Martha finally understood that God's tests had been just that —a way to prove her faith, her endurance, her patience.

And Joshua had been her rock, her foundation, all along. There was no doubt in her mind now that they were truly meant to be together.

"We didn't want to wait for another catastrophe to hit and deter us again," Martha quipped.

"Isn't life just one big catastrophe, though?" Joanna sighed, catching the end of their conversation. She grinned sheepishly. "I'm sorry. That's not very optimistic for a wedding, is it?"

Martha returned her smile and took her hand. "You have been through too much," she offered the young woman. "You're entitled to a bit of pessimism. But don't forget that it's always darkest before the dawn."

Joanna squeezed her hand as Joshua made his way through the crowd toward them. "I think I saw some butter tarts over there. I'm going to sneak one before Eliza eats them all," Joanna joked, ducking away.

"Is she having a *gut* time?" Joshua asked, watching Joanna wander off toward the food.

"I can't tell," Martha answered honestly, and Joshua laughed.

"I hope so," he murmured, ducking his head close to her ear. A shiver rushed through her as his breath warmed her cheek. "But this day is about you and me."

Carefully, he guided her around the corner, away from the

bustle of the festivities, and instantly nuzzled against Martha's neck.

"There are children around!" Martha teased, but she did not pull away.

"You have made me the happiest mann alive today, Martha," he whispered into her neck. "I have dreamed of this day for longer than I care to admit."

She cocked her head back and peered at him. "Longer than I think?" she asked shyly.

He nodded. "Not that I would have ever done anything to disrespect you or Peter. I cared for both of you much, too much for that."

With shining eyes, Martha cupped his face and brought her husband's lips to hers. The sweet shock of his kiss warmed her from head to toe, floating Martha heavenward. They parted, but kept their noses close.

"There is *nix* we can't handle with *Gott* on our side," Martha promised him.

"*Nee*. Not as long as we're together," Joshua agreed.

~*~*~

Click here to get your copy of 'An Amish Gift of Love - 10 Book Box Set' - Today!

Sample of Chapter One

The light from the fireplace cast shadows over the bedroom walls as Susanna King strained against the bedding.

"Lie back, Susie," Amos urged. "Don't push yourself."

Her hand clutched her husband's, their fingers twined as tightly as she could muster, but his hold was much firmer than hers. She simply did not have the strength, much as she tried to hold on. He touched her face with his free hand, stroking her cheek sweetly, his eyes locking on hers.

"*Pliese,* Susie," Amos begged quietly as to not rouse the attention of their son who lingered in the hallway. "You must fight harder. You can't let this sickness take you."

Susanna smiled wanly, her once-lovely face sallow and graying, fading away like the autumn sunshine.

"I've done my best," she breathed, her words wispy. "But I don't think I can do much more. *Gott* is calling me to Him. I don't think I can hold off much longer, *liebling*."

Amos shook his head vehemently.

"*Nee*! It's not time yet. Levi needs his *mudder*. I need my *weib*!"

She sank deeper into the pillows, her frail face nearly disappearing among the linens.

"I wish I could stay and watch Levi become the *mann* he is meant to be, a strapping, hard-working *mann* like you and Sam," she mumbled, her voice fading slightly with the effort. All this talk was draining her and Amos stifled his pleas.

They did little but ply her with guilt, but what was Susanna to do? She had fought as hard as she could for months. She deserved peace and rest now. Why could he not let her go with grace and ease?

"*Mamm*?" Levi called from the hallway. "Can I *kumme* inside?"

"*Nee,* Levi!" Amos choked, holding his hands up to ward his young son back. "Your *mudder* needs her rest. Leave her in peace!"

"Tsk, Amos," Susanna rasped softly, her words catching in the thick of her congested chest. "Let him *kumme*."

Tears blinded Amos' pale blue eyes, but he willed himself not to shed them as he held his wife's gaze.

"Amos…"

Dr. James cleared his throat discretely from the hallway at Levi's side, nodding for Amos to follow him into the hallway. Amos was reluctant to leave his ailing wife's side, but he could not refuse the doctor's request. The local practitioner had been at the King home over the past several days as Susanna's condition grew worse, her prognosis undeniable. A part of the young man did not want to hear whatever the English doctor would have to say, but he could not disrespect Dr. James by ignoring his request for a moment.

"Samuel," Amos called to his brother, who waited on the main floor. "*Kumme* and be with Susanna."

"Me too, *Daed*?" Levi begged. "I would like to stay too!"

"*Nee,*" Amos said sharply. "You will ready yourself for bed. The hour is late and you have *schul* in the *mariye*."

"*Daed—*" the boy started to argue, but a simple look from his distraught father silenced him into submission.

"Levi," Susanna called weakly from the bedroom. "*Kumme,* say *guten nacht* to me first, *mein sohn.*"

Swallowing thickly, Amos allowed the boy to scamper toward his mother, curls bouncing freely as he passed by his father without so much as a second look. Samuel appeared on the second floor, his face pale and drawn from days of little sleep, the shifts of watching over Susanna taking their toll on him as well.

"Watch over Susanna a moment while I speak with the *doktor,*" Amos mumbled, gesturing for his older brother to sit with his wife.

"We'll make coffee," Dr. James suggested with forced brightness, guiding the way downstairs.

Amos had no interest in drinking coffee or leaving the second floor at all, but he took small comfort in knowing that his brother would stay with his wife while he attended to Dr. James.

"You need to take breaks, Amos," Dr. James told him chidingly. "It's not healthy for you to stay cooped up in the house all the time."

Amos eyed the well-meaning man warily.

"I don't want to be far from Susanna, should she need anything," he explained.

The good doctor nodded, pulling out a chair at the kitchen table, causing the lit lantern on the table to flicker with his movement. He sighed deeply before sitting, avoiding Amos' pointed stare.

"I understand that, Amos, but you will only run yourself ragged and, frankly, my friend, Susanna doesn't have much more time. The cancer has ravaged her body. You're going to need your strength."

"You've said that many times over the last week!" Amos cried indignantly, not wanting to hear his words. Dr. James eyed him patiently, knowing that Amos spoke only with emotion.

"Only God can say for sure when her time has truly come, Amos, but you must know it's near."

It did not matter how many people prepared him for this end, for this loss, he would never be ready to say goodbye to his wife of only eight years. They had committed to a life together, one filled with children. They had only welcomed one son before the cancer had come and ruined their plans for the future.

"Come now, Amos. Let's get that coffee going, shall we?" Dr. James prompted. "It's bound to be another long night.

Levi wanted nothing more but to crawl into his mother's arms, but Samuel stopped him, alarmed by the frailty of his brother's wife. He worried that even the slightest weight would break Susanna.

"A small hug will suffice, Levi," Samuel told him. "Then, you heard what your *vadder* said—off to bed you go."

"Give me a kiss, Levi," Susanna implored him, her cerulean eyes wide and sad. Samuel's gut lurched, a terrible sense of foreboding gripping his stomach as he noted the pallor of her face. Over the past days, the life and color had faded away to a terrible, waxen shade, the veins visible beneath her flesh. The vibrant young woman who had chased Levi through the King farm was hardly recognizable, but for the pretty cornflower blue of her eyes.

Samuel swallowed the lump in his throat as his nephew obliged his mother, reluctantly lingering in the doorway as though he, too, could sense the dark cloud that hung lower than it had ever hung in the bedroom.

"*Guten nacht, mein sohn,*" Susanna whispered.

"*Guten nacht, Mamm,*" Levi replied, turning to leave his uncle and mother alone in the bedroom. Once she was certain the boy was out of earshot, Susanna gestured for Samuel to come closer. Instantly, Samuel sprung from the wing chair and crouched by her side.

"What is it?" he asked worriedly. "Would you like *wasser*? Should I send for Amos?"

She shook her head, tongue jutting out slightly to wet her cracked lips.

"Sam," she murmured. "I need you to make me a promise."

"Susanna, you must rest," Samuel told her, guessing the conversation was about to take a darker turn. "Promises are for another day. It's late—"

"Sam, there are no other days," she rasped, every word sounding painful to utter. Samuel's heart began to pound as Susanna reached for his hand and he glanced helplessly toward the door, hoping that his brother might return with the doctor. He had no illusions as to Susanna's health, but he also had not expected her to take such an abrupt turn in minutes.

"*Pliese,* Sam," she begged. "Listen to me."

He choked back his protests, knowing that he was hearing a dying woman's final requests, and nodded, silently urging her to go on, despite his reservations.

"You must promise to look after your *bruder* and Levi. I-I don't think they will survive well without you."

Samuel's opaque blue eyes popped, sadness overwhelming him.

"Promise me!" Susanna implored him again, demanding that he give an answer.

"I will always be here for my *familye,* Susie, of course. I don't need to tell you that."

She relaxed, a smile touching her pale lips as she fell back on the pillow, shoulders sagging.

"*Gut,*" she murmured. "That's *gut*."

Her eyes closed then, a long, even breath escaping her lungs, but that was the last one she would ever exhale. A gasp shook Samuel's body and his lips parted to cry out for his brother, but he immediately clamped them closed, terrified of rousing his nephew. He did not want Levi to see his mother lifeless.

Tears sprang to his eyes, and he buried his face in his hands, his lanky frame rocking until the sound of footfalls lifted his head and he stared at his brother with streaked cheeks. Horror crossed over Amos' stricken face, his gaze darting from Samuel to his wife, the wind knocking from him as he collapsed to his knees.

"*Nee*! Susanna, *nee*! *Pliese, Gott*!"

His wails permeated the walls of the house, stirring Levi from his room, but Samuel caught the boy before he could run inside, clinging to the seven-year-old's shoulders as he struggled to reach his mother.

"*Nee, sohn,*" he mumbled, grief overtaking him, making his voice hoarse and thick. "You don't want to remember your *mudder* like that. Think of her in the fields, picking *blumme.* Remember her knitting your hats for the winter. Do not recall her lying in bed, sick and frail. She wouldn't want that."

The boy's body trembled violently, his slender frame folding against his uncle's, and Samuel stroked Levi's thick curls tenderly, remembering his promise to Susanna.

I will always be here for you, he vowed silently. *We will make it through this together, as a familye.*

A NOTE FROM THE AUTHOR

Dear Reader,

I do hope that you enjoyed reading **'The Amish Foundling Finds Love'**

Possibly you even identify with the characters in some small way. Many of us presume to know God's will for our lives, and don't realize that His timing often does not match our own.

The foremost reason that I love writing about the Amish is that their lifestyle is diametrically opposed to the Western norm. The simplicity and purity evident there is so vastly refreshing that the story lines derived from them are suitable for everyone.

Be sure to keep an eye out for the next book which is coming soon.

Emma Cartwright

Thank You!

Thank you for purchasing this book. We hope that you have enjoyed reading it.

If you enjoyed reading this book **please may you consider**

leaving a review — it really would help greatly to get the word out!

~

Newsletter

If you love reading sweet, clean, Amish Romance stories why not join Emma Cartwright's newsletter and receive advance notification of new releases and more!

Simply sign up here: http://eepurl.com/dgw2I5

And get your ***FREE*** copy of **Amish Unexpected Love**

~

Contact Me

If you'd simply like to drop us a line you can contact us at **emma@emmacartwrightauthor.com**

You can also connect with me on my new **Facebook page**.

I will always let you know about new releases on my Facebook page, so it is worth liking that if you get the chance.

LIKE EMMA'S FB PAGE HERE

I welcome your thoughts and would love to hear from you!

I will then also be able to let you know about new books coming out along with Amazon special deals etc

Made in the USA
Monee, IL
03 October 2024

67179711R00059